Conte~

1

Chapter 1:
Dangerous and daring: now (Jem)

I wasn't sure when it began or how I managed to get into this situation, but the first thing I remember when I look in the rearview mirror of my little Peugeot 207 was that I had gotten myself into a bit of a pickle. My ivory silk off-the-shoulder wedding dress is slightly creased from being bunched to fit into the front seat of the car and red blotches have formed around my neck and cheeks. My eyeliner and mascara has smudged so much I look as if I have two black eyes and my short, curly dark hair looks a mess. The hair clips keeping my birdcage veil in place are hanging precariously askew, like an acupuncture session gone wrong, and, for the hundredth time today, I wished that I had more controllable hair. *"For goodness sake, Jem, get a grip on yourself,"* I say to no one there. *"You look like you've been dragged through a hedge backwards."* Quickly, I pull out the hair clips and pull at the veil to free my unruly mop. Now, that feels much better.

So, back to my predicament, yes – I am currently sitting in my car in a wedding dress, on the verge of a complete meltdown, having left my would-be husband standing in the registry office among his family and our friends. "Shit...shit...shit..." I mutter. It's hard to be stoical when all you want to do is to burst into tears – but I am trying here. First thing though, I need to start driving and get as far away from here as I possibly could so that I can think straight and work out my next steps. I find the spare key, hidden in my well thought through hiding place in the glove compartment, and turn on the ignition. I put the car into gear and take off the handbrake when a fist bangs against the driver's side window. *Fuck! It's Craig, the ditched groom and he looks mad as hell.*

"What the hell, Jem! Get out of the car and face me. What's going on with you?"

Craig keeps one hand on the top of the roof of the car, as if he thinks this will stop me from leaving. His face is red and matches his red ruffled spiky hair, he looks as though he's had electric shock treatment and the current is still on. I stare at him in all his wedding finery, trying to think why I believed I could trust and love this man in the first place. He wasn't really my type…but then what was my type, someone with dark hair and blue eyes?

Thinking back, there was always a feeling of dishonesty about him, but I couldn't quite put my finger on why I felt this way. So, in the end, I got swept away with the excitement of finally having someone to love in my life, and to finally having someone to love me for being me.

My instincts are to open the door and kick him in the balls or to do some clever martial arts move to his face. Whichever causes the most pain. Thankfully, I keep my instincts in check and take a deep breath. I stare at him, angry with him for being such a dick, and with myself for getting caught up in his web of lies that involve having contact with my mother.

He attempts to pull open the door, but I shake my head sadly and slowly start to drive. I drive as tears roll down my cheeks and I sigh with relief as my hands and feet respond automatically. I find myself heading to the only place that I think no one will look for me and that I have ever felt safe in my life. Shore House.

I can almost hear my mother's shrill voice shouting, *"Jemima, what has gotten into you? How dare you do this to me, I'll be a laughing stock."*

"Yes, you and me both, Mother," I grimace to myself. *"You and me both."*

Is it too late to finally rid oneself of the fear that has haunted you for most of your life? Can I find the strength to move forward and be the happy, carefree, independent person who I feel I deserve to be? Well, I have made the first daring step, something that not even my clever mother would have dreamed in her wildest dreams that I would do. I have taken myself away from the danger, from the poison and from those who wish me harm, and now I am heading for my safe place. No "congratulations to the bride and groom", no wedding speeches and no sharing a hopeful future with someone who cares for me. Thanks for nothing, Craig.

I pull onto the side of the road, I need to clear my head. I have no money, no mobile and no clothes. Clearly, I haven't thought this through very well. *If you're going to do a runner, better to have your essentials planned well in advance.* Yes, well, hindsight is a wonderful thing! Luckily, there is a full tank of diesel in my car or my runaway bride moment might have been very short-lived. Many years ago I'd had friends who lived in the Weymouth area and I decided to pin my hopes on a friend called Maureen still being alive. Surely, she will take pity on a bedraggled bride-dressed urchin in need of a bed for the night and a stiff drink.

I lose track of time as I move automatically through the mechanics of driving the car and making the monotonous journey toward my destination. My thoughts focus entirely on getting to the Dorset coast safely and, secondly, on the need to hide from the outside world. Slowly the familiar signs and roads take shape, leaving me feeling relieved and emotional. I shuffle around in my seat, trying to move the bottom half of the wedding dress. It's become tight in parts and a little uncomfortable to drive in.

I didn't even know if Maureen was alive or if she still lived in the same house. So many thoughts, questions and scenarios whizz around my frantic mind until suddenly a detached calmness comes over me. Finally, I park outside the old cottage and take a deep breath. "Don't worry, it will be okay," I murmur to myself as I take the keys out of the ignition, get out of the car and walk to the familiar green gate with surprisingly overgrown weeds. Maureen used to keep her garden in such good order. She always had a neat lawn, bright-coloured flowers bursting from smart little pots, all smartly presented, but I guess she is a lot older now and things change. It is dusk as I press the doorbell and wait.

Maureen answers the door, and we both stare at each other. She hasn't changed, well, apart from the colour of her hair. She's tall, robust and cuddly with a mop of shoulder-length grey hair framing her face.

"Aunty Maureen," I say throwing myself into her arms.

"Jemima, I knew you would come back," she says hugging me tightly. Why couldn't my mother have been like this? I think sadly. Would it have hurt her to have shown me some affection once in a while? Maureen pulls away, holds me at arm's length, and takes a good look at the wedding dress.

"Got yourself in a bit of trouble then, young lady?" I nod, then smile for the first time in what seems like forever. Maureen was always one for stating the obvious.

"Well, I take it you're staying for a bit then. I'd better make up the spare bed and get you out of that dress," she said, staring at me with determination.

I slump into the nearest armchair, car keys still in my hand. What does a person do when she hits rock bottom? My mind is spiralling with thoughts of what I had done and why I had done it. I don't want my body to shut down, but I am exhausted and can't think straight. I hear a movement as Maureen comes toward me clutching what looks like spare clothes in her hands and thrusts them at me.

"Here you go, dear."

I stand up just as the front door opens and a ghost from my past stands in front of me, a ghost with dark hair and deep blue eyes. Then everything goes black.

Chapter 2:
Can bananas cry?: ten years ago (Jem)

"Jemima, come down here this instant!" I can't find my pencil case for school and am crawling around on my hands and knees looking under my bed. Oh no, what does she want now? I spy the pencil case which had fallen off my desk and lay wedged between my bed and the desk, pick it up and throw it into my school bag.

"Hurry up, girl, you're going to be late for school."

I wish I knew what her problem was, my mother is always on my case and not always in a good way. "Coming," I shout, rushing down the stairs. As I enter the kitchen to see what she wants something heavy catches me on the side of my head. Stunned and a bit wobbly, I look at Mother with disbelief. "What the hell?" I massage my head and stare at the heavy silver saucepan still in her hand.

"You could have killed me!" I say, shaking my head vigorously to get rid of the stars floating before my eyes. I step away from her quickly. Clearly, she is not having a good day today. *When does she ever?* I think to myself. *Of all the women in the world to have as a mother I have to have her. Deranged. Selfish. Violent. Uncaring. Yes, that's my mother. As mentally unstable as they come. And she's all mine!*

"What did you think you were doing, telling your teacher that you slipped and fell in the shower? I found a note in your homework diary." Clearly, I needed to tell him something, when a fifteen year old is wearing a long-sleeved school shirt in the height of summer and he tells you to roll up your sleeves, where you reveal several bruise marks and a variety of cuts. Trying to avoid complications is my life's work and trying to avoid unwanted attention from physical abuse is definitely a work in progress.

"It's the first thing that I could think of to explain the marks on my arms," I mutter, rubbing my head and keeping within an arm's length of her being able to reach me.

The doorbell rings and I go to answer it. Thankfully, it's my best friend Noah standing there peeping in and trying to distract my mum. "Ready?" he asks, looking at me as though he knows that something's happened. I grab my stuff and head out the door, collecting a banana on the way.

"What's up with her?" he mutters. "She's got that wild look again…has she hurt you?"

"No," I mutter absently, rubbing the side of my head. He takes my shoulder and twists me so that I face him, deep blue eyes search mine as he gently cups the side of my cheek. He looks scared, defeated and angry. For a long moment our eyes lock in acceptance and despair. Then he whispers in a low voice.

"Jesus, one of these days she's going to really hurt you, Jem. You need to tell someone, or I will."

Subconsciously I hold onto my banana as if it were a lifeline, digging my fingernails into its flesh to keep my emotions in check. *Don't be kind to me, Noah, not now when*

I'm trying so hard to hold myself together. My life was a joke, what did I do to deserve such incompetent parents? A father who left to "find himself" when I was four years old, and a mother who couldn't forgive him and saw the world and everyone in it as her enemy. Perhaps she will mellow with age I ponder as I feel the sticky flesh of the banana seep through my fingers. Yes, and perhaps bananas cry!

"It's not that bad, she's just angry all of the time. Mostly with me. Since Dad left she blames me for things that go wrong, and with her things go wrong a lot. Usually I'm more guarded and faster when deflecting the slaps and missiles. But this morning I was running late because I couldn't find my pencil case and I wasn't thinking straight, wasn't fast enough."

"Don't." He shakes his head.

"Don't what?" I ask.

"Don't defend her."

He let go of my cheek. He knew it wouldn't help to say anything to her, if anything it would probably make it worse. I was too young to get my own place and needed to stay in school for another year. The only person who really looked out for me, apart from Noah, was my mum's ex-friend Maureen who lived a few streets away.

When they were friends my mum used to tell me to call Maureen "Aunty Maureen" – as if she were part of the family. I usually go there after school, do my homework and sip the tea and biscuits that she gives me without asking. She also gives me dinner to make sure that I'm not hungry by the time I get home. Mum doesn't get back from work until six, so my timings need to work like clockwork each school day; rush to Maureen's with Noah, where we make a start on our homework, have an early dinner at 5pm and unwind briefly before I head home at 5.30pm to tidy the house and start dinner. Maureen gives me something else that my mother cannot – she gives me unconditional love. Noah, well, he gives me friendship and stability and a calmness that I don't have anywhere else in my life. Oh, and did I remember to say? Noah is Maureen's grandson.

Noah and I arrive at class and say our goodbyes until lunchtime. I throw my demolished breakfast banana in the bin as I make my way into my form room. My fingers are sticky with banana mulch and I give them a quick wash in a nearby water fountain. I take one last look at Noah as he chats to his friend Charlie and watch as they walk through the main school library door. There is an odd fluttering in my chest as I think of Noah and there's a little hollow feeling in my stomach from lack of breakfast. I take my usual seat at the back of the class and try to hide my rumbling tummy as my teacher, Mr Edwards, calls the register. Yep, it's just another day in this crazy life of mine.

Chapter 3:
Some kind of sticky toffee pudding: now (Jem)

I wake in a strange room. The curtains are closed, and I am unsure of the time. I peek under the duvet and discover that I am no longer wearing my wedding dress. I breathe a sigh of relief. I don't want any reminders of what I've just done. I'm assuming and sort of hoping that Maureen had undressed me and that's why I am wearing a long flannelette pink flowery nightdress. I can hear voices, I think, from the rooms below. Soft voices, there's one with a deep tone to it. Noah.

"Did she say anything?" he asks.

"Nothing. Just turned up and threw herself at me. Something bad has happened. I can feel it in her. I've never known a person have as much bad luck as that girl. That mother of hers has something to do with it – I'm pretty sure of it. Whenever Jemima got hurt or ill the mum was always behind it. That's why we're no longer friends. I told her to stop hurting and belittling the girl. I told her I wouldn't stand by and watch her doing that to her child anymore. You can see how well that went…"

The voices lower and I struggle to hear the rest of the conversation. There is movement below me then all goes quiet.

Slowly I sit up and shuffle to the side of the bed ignoring the light-headedness that suddenly swoops through me. I shake my head vigorously, trying to clear the fog as I move carefully to the door. All of a sudden it swings open.

"Thought you were awake," Noah says, as he pauses in the doorway. "I can hear you moving about. You've been asleep for two hours and it's nearly 8pm."

I take a long look at him. He has changed. There's a confident, slightly harsh look about him, but I can still see the young carefree, easy-going Noah just below the surface. Although he is tall and solid, he isn't heavily muscled. His dark brown hair is short and neat and the black T-shirt and grey jeans make him look casual and comfortable in his own skin. More than I can say for me.

"Noah…" I begin. I don't know what to say. We haven't seen each other in ten years and the circumstances which took me away from all the things and people that mattered to me lay heavily on my mind.

My legs feel weak and begin to buckle beneath me but I'm not surprised, I haven't eaten anything for nearly twenty-four hours. I need sustenance and quickly, I tell myself, as I grope for something to hold on to. I wait for the ground to swallow me but instead a pair of strong arms lift me and scoop me back to the bed. He sits on the bed, a look of concern on his face as he absently tucks a stray hair behind my ear.

"Of all the times I pictured seeing you again, this was never one of them," he grinds out, as if to himself.

"I'm so mad at you for the way you disappeared on me."

"I know. And, I'm sorry" – I have to say it, of all the things that I have regretted in my life, leaving Noah, losing Noah, is the biggest of all. Still, I had been in an intolerable, abusive relationship with my mother and she had been the one and only reason for me leaving home at fifteen.

"Jem, I haven't seen you in ten years. You didn't write or call, you didn't try to make any contact. I thought you were dead. Shit, Jem. I can't get my head around this. You. Here. Now. Of all times!" He pushes his hand through his hair.

He stands up, leaves the room and I stare at the open door, wondering if he'll return. He comes back a few minutes later carrying a tea tray bustling with objects.

"Gran told me to give you this." He sets the tray on the bed, picks up a large mug, adds sugar and milk and puts it on the bedside table. I look at the steaming cup of tea and feel calmer as I watch him put a bowl of something that has a very familiar aroma next to the cup.

I peek over and take in the sticky toffee pudding and the slowly melting ice cream and close my eyes. Maureen knows me well. Memories flood my mind of a little girl never quite fed enough at home, in need of good, sweet things to bring light into the darkness, reminding me of the old Julie Andrews song, "Raindrops on Roses".

I was ten years old when I began cooking dinner for myself and Mother at home. She filled the fridge and cupboards in her own haphazard way, when she remembered. Before this she would often forget about me and bring in takeaways which she would eat in front of me but not offer one morsel. Thank God for Maureen. Carefully, I look at Noah – we need to talk but I'm afraid, afraid that he won't understand. That he won't forgive me. I bolster every ounce of confidence I can and take the lead.

"Noah, when I've settled down I'd really like to talk to you and Maureen and explain what happened. I know it's in the past, but I need you both to know that I'm not some heartless person who leaves those who care for her behind without a single thought."

Brooding, he bends down so his face is almost touching mine, and before I know what is happening I feel his lips press lightly on mine. It breaks as quickly as it starts, and I feel confused and elated at the same time.

"It's too late, Jem. You're too late." He shakes his head sadly and makes for the door.

"We'll be downstairs when you're ready to talk."

Suddenly the tea and pudding doesn't seem so appetising. My mouth feels dry, but I force the hot sweet liquid down my throat and ponder. What does he mean? Why am I too late? My problems are mounting so high that I figure they must be unsolvable by now. I had hoped to re-think my options and find some sort of peace here, but maybe this was what I was meant to be doing. Perhaps, I am meant to go back through my past to close the doors properly so that I can open them again to begin a happy, healthy future.

I find some leggings and a sweatshirt sitting on a nearby chair and pull them on. Slowly, I make my way downstairs to confront my demons and to begin to rebuild my shattered life.

Chapter 4:
Mad with power: then (Jem)

What most people don't know about me is that I love drawing and painting. I am always doodling or sketching something or other. Noah watches me doodling, often smiling as the sketches develop and slowly fill my small notebook. My drawing is mine; something that my mother can't sully in any way.

At twelve I knew even then that there would come a time when I would need to make the break away from my mother – sooner rather than later. Now I am fifteen and fighting for my very existence. I knew there was a malice in her, and could see the anger always simmering making her ready to lash out. The power she used to control almost every aspect of my life was too much, suffocating. I didn't feel safe in any part of my life apart from when I was with Noah, Maureen or in my bedroom. I needed to take control before it was too late. I had put together an escape bag with a few clothes, including nightwear, useful information, phone numbers, birthday spare cash that I had managed to hide in an old sock in my lower bedside drawer and some destinations and ideas for getting away safely. If I had to leave quickly this was my "escape" plan.

I had been to Maureen's house where Noah and I had done our homework and then had dinner. I'd rushed home to tidy the house and start dinner. At 6.10pm, Mother arrived home. My peace was shattered and my senses were on high alert. I could smell the alcohol on her from the kitchen as she walks toward me.

"I'm home!" she announced as though I was blind and couldn't see her. Just at that moment the door pushed open behind her and a tall older man wearing a cheap-looking suit, about fiftyish and bald, came into the kitchen.

Immediately, alarm bells rang. This was new, even for her.

"Jemima, this is Pete – a friend of mine from work."

"You didn't tell me she was so pretty," said Old Pete, looking me up and down. "Jemima is it?" he said, putting his hand out.

I didn't take the hand but nodded. "Pete."

"Don't be silly. She's not pretty. Jemima takes after her father, she's difficult and challenging. A real handful. I try my best but she's hard work." Mother's voice had started to whine. I tried hard not to roll my eyes.

"I'm going to change into something more comfortable," Mother babbles as she heads for the door. "We'll have dinner in ten minutes. Have it ready on the table for then," she adds, looking my way.

An awkward silence fills the air. I mash the potatoes and check on the sausages sizzling in the oven. I am mentally wondering if there is enough food to feed another person when a movement behind me catches me unawares. Old Pete starts stroking my neck.

"Do you mind?" I ask, moving away.

"No, your mother said that you were feisty and I like that in a woman." *But I'm not really a woman, I think, gritting my teeth. I'm not a grown woman, I'm fifteen!*

17

I finish mashing the potatoes and there it is again, only this time his hand starts stroking my back and is moving lower. I turn around in an instant and before I can stop myself I smash the potato masher into his face. Hard. The red imprints from the masher stare back at me as I yell, "Get the fuck off me, you pervert!"

Before I can move out of his grasp his hands have me by the throat.

"You fucking bitch! Who the fuck do you think you are? I will fucking show you how to behave with your mum's friends."

"Pete! What are you doing?" came my mother's shrill voice as she walks into the kitchen carrying a bottle of wine and two glasses.

"Teaching your fucking daughter some manners." He shrugs letting go of my neck.

"Get the dinner on the table, Jemima. We're hungry." The person who is supposed to protect me sits down at the dining table stroking Old Pete's arm and gushing at him. How can I live with someone who wields so much power in my life and uses that power to hurt and debase me? Every child and young person is entitled to feel safe in his or her own home. I wasn't. I cannot, and will not, let someone have abusive power over me.

To say dinner was strained is an understatement. Watching my mother and Old Pete drinking, kissing and stroking each other's hands and faces was enough to make me heave. I really wasn't hungry. Still, I played it cool and went through the

18

motions until it was time to clear the dinner dishes away. I went to my room, put the chair against the door and began to put my escape plan into action. I dressed in several layers of clothes and tried hard to block out the progressively louder grunts and panting coming from Mother's room. It made me feel sick.

Slowly, and as quietly as I could, I removed the chair from blocking the door. I took one last look at the room that had been my sanctuary since birth, hurled my escape bag onto my shoulders and opened my bedroom door. I walked across the landing to the steps. They were still making grunting noises and something hard, like the bedframe, was knocking into the wall. At the bottom of the stairs I grabbed my mobile and coat and quietly opened the front door.

Stage one complete.

Chapter 5:
Don't let me fall: now (Jem)

Maureen is knitting in her chair. There is something reassuring to see that she still likes to knit, though I'm not sure why that is. Noah is pacing the floor. He looks as if he's ready to kill someone…that would probably be me.

I slowly sit down on the sofa and lean my arms on my knees.

"I owe you both so much," I begin, clenching my hands together to stop them from shaking.

"I have done things that I am not proud of, like walking out on you, Noah." I look quickly at him, not willing to meet his eyes. "And, not letting you know where I was or that I was safe. But there are a few things I need to do first. Maureen, can you please contact Jenny at The Lighthouse? Tell her that I'm here and that I have been compromised. She'll know what to do."

Noah looks baffled as Maureen moves toward the phone. The lack of understanding is beginning to frustrate him as he raises his voice.

"Slow down, Jem, I don't understand. What is this place, The Lighthouse? Who the is hell is Jenny?"

Maureen stands still. I nod to her and she sits down again.

"Noah, I once told you many years ago that there would come a time when things would need to change, that I might need to get away from my mother. Something happened one night, something that made me believe that escape was the only option."

Noah sits down next to me on the sofa.

"I'm listening," he says slowly in a quiet voice.

In the same quiet voice, I tell him about the night that Old Pete came to the house and what had happened. I tell him of the potato masher incident and the events that led me to leave the house that night and to never go back. He looks angry, I hope his anger is directed at my mother and Old Pete rather than me. He mumbles something that sounds like "Fucking bitch" to himself. I want to reach out to him, to say that it wasn't his fault, that he had always tried to help me where he could. This was my decision, my choice, and whether it was right or wrong, it was me fighting for survival at fifteen the only way I could – fight or flight. There wasn't really an option, was there?

Maureen catches my eye and I nod to her.

"Noah, what Jemima didn't tell you was that she came to me for help first. She had her reasons and was desperate to make herself disappear."

"To you? What do you mean she came to you? For god's sake, Gran, you knew how much she meant to me, you saw how upset I was when she disappeared. Now you're telling me that she came to you and you knew what had happened!" He pushes up from the sofa and moves toward her chair, brooding.

"How could you? How could you do that and not let me know that she was okay?"

"It's not her fault, Noah. It's mine. Please listen, I'm trying to tell you what happened. I want you to understand," I say, defending Maureen and pleading with Noah.

"I understand alright. You didn't trust me enough to confide in me. You made the decisions between you to keep me in the dark. I feel like a fool, a complete bloody fool."

"Noah! That's enough!" Maureen's raised voice made us both look at her. She never raises her voice. "You need to listen to Jemima and hear what she has to say."

Noah moves away and sits himself on the farthest end of the sofa from me as possible. His face is set in stone, showing no emotion as he defensively crosses his arms. I know he's in shock and that his pride is hurt, but I need to tell him the rest of the story.

"I was going to get on a bus. It was dark and wet outside. My plan had been to get the number fifty-seven to the railway station, then get a ticket for the first train that was due in on the platform. I didn't care where it was going or how long the journey. Then, I realised that at fifteen, I was putting myself in more danger just by travelling alone at night.

"So, instead I came to Maureen's. We talked and thought about the safest options and then she admitted that she knew someone who had put her in touch with a charity who offered refuge for women and children who were experiencing domestic violence abuse. They have two refuge facilities, which they call 'refuge homes', hidden in the Dorset and Hampshire areas.

"Maureen called them as an emergency. I knew that mother would think that I'd run to you or Maureen and wanted to keep you both out of her poisonous clutches. Jenny answered the call and came within an hour. Jenny was really kind, she listened to my story about Mother, the abuse and the constant living threat of violence, and we all agreed that it would be safer to move me to one of the refuge homes.

"Jenny knew that this was a really unusual situation. More often, she would place mother and child or children together in one of the homes and they would have been referred to them by the police or social services. With me, I couldn't risk Mother finding me, even through you or Maureen. It was the only way."

Noah looks at Maureen and then at me. He gives a huge sigh. The silence seems to last forever. I feel exhausted. I just want to sleep. Noah moves to sit next to me. I stay still, waiting to see what he will do. He needs to make the first move. I am not begging. I feel his arm slip around my shoulder, his hand gripping me firmly and he lets out a huge sigh. I didn't realise that I'd been holding my breath as I slump into him. He turns my chin to face him and his blue eyes hold mine.

"We're not fifteen anymore, Jem, and there is no way in this lifetime that I am letting you walk away again. We're grown up now and, yes, we have different lives – but we will sort it out. I promise."

"Noah, I am not your responsibility!" I state getting a little riled by his caveman-like approach to dealing with my life problems. "I do not need you to tell me what I can and can't do."

I pull away from him. Maureen stands up.

"Jemima, he doesn't mean it that way, you know he doesn't. I'm going to phone Jenny, she'll know what to do," she says, heading into the hall.

Then I stand too. I stare into the darkness through the windows, looking at the light shining from the lamp-post at the front of the house.

"Sometimes I see the world and the world sees me, but they're totally different. The lamp-post shines like a beacon to guide the way home. You can shake it, but it doesn't move. Have you ever done that? Stood at the bottom of the lamp-post when it's dark, looked up into the bright light and tried to shake the post? The cool metal is strong. It stands proud. Isolated, but part of the world. The same but different. You keep shaking it. Nothing happens. Sometimes there are people out there who keep chipping away at you, trying to knock you down or worse. It's hard and it's weary, staying firm, standing tall, not letting anyone shake you. I feel like I'm the lamp-post. It's stupid, I know."

I don't realise I'm talking aloud until I feel arms slide around my shoulders. Noah's scent hits me.

"I see you, Jem. I see who you are."

"Don't let me fall, Noah. I left once, to start again and to survive. I've built a life of independence, a careful life where I could live safely and hopefully one day find love and have a family of my own. Then I find...Oh shit, it's all such a bloody mess."

"I don't care. The mess, any of it. I don't care. You came back to us. We will find a way through this. Whatever has happened, is happening or will happen, we will deal with it, one day at a time. And, Jem, one more thing…"

I turn my head to look at him.

"If you fall, I will catch you."

The tears fall down my cheeks.

Maureen's voice interrupts the silence. "Jenny says she'll pop by for breakfast tomorrow around 8.30am. She says she's bringing pastries and to have strong coffee ready." She shadows the doorframe, unsure whether to enter the room.

Noah looks at us both. "I'm going to head home. You need to rest, Jem, you look beat. Gran, walk me to the door, will you?" They move quietly toward the front door, talking as they go.

So, here I am building bridges, facing my demons and wondering what on earth I have begun by coming back to my roots. One thing's for sure though. This is the first time I've given any thought about the wedding that wasn't and that stupid prick Craig. That's got to be a good thing, right?

Chapter 6:
In the blink of an eye: then (Noah)

Reader, I married him.

"This is one of the most memorable phrases of *Jane Eyre*. Why do you think that Charlotte Bronte writes in the first person?"

I'm not really listening to Mrs Chapman our English teacher as we discuss how to use different creative writing techniques and prose. I'm still hung up on Jem and her mother. How could a mother do that to her own child? The situation is escalating. At first it was just nasty comments dropped into a sentence, but then the bruises and cuts started to appear. The occasional split lip that was always the result of walking into a door. Everything about her mother made me feel uncomfortable.

"Noah! At least try to pretend that you are listening."

"Sorry, Miss. Got a bit of a headache," I lie trying to cover my tracks. I am worried about Jem and cannot shake the thought that something bad is about to happen. My gaze moves to Jem sitting at the far side of the room. She is making notes, scribbling and probably doing the odd doodle. Absently she rubs the side of her head. I feel so angry that I wish I had something equally as heavy as the saucepan so that I could give that bitch mother Joyce a taste of her own medicine.

Jem puts her hand up.

"Yes, Jemima?"

"Using the first person can make the character feel more real, intimate and more engaged, but you can do that with third person narratives too, surely? This book, it feels like an autobiography."

"I like your thoughts, Jemima. You're right of course, a good writer can easily use the third person to create intimate and engaging scenes and scenarios. Good feedback." Jem smiles, she's pleased that Mrs Chapman likes her comments.

I'm going to speak to Gran tonight and see what she thinks about Jem and her home situation. She was friends with Joyce years ago and she may have some ideas about how to help Jem. I fire a quick text to my mum and tell her that I'll be a little late home from Gran's tonight. I know that Jem nearly always has dinner with Gran, sometimes I do too – depends on homework and what time Mum gets home from work.

There's a nudge to my leg and my mate Charlie whispers, "Hey, Noe, fancy hanging out tonight?"

"Sorry, mate, tomorrow? I've got something I need to do tonight."

"No problem, mate. We can do it tomorrow. Come over to mine and we'll order pizza and watch a film."

"Sounds good," I whisper.

My mind wanders back to Jem. The other thing that's bugging me is that it's getting harder for me to hide my feelings for her. In all the time I have known Jem I have wanted to protect her and be the one she turns to, needs and trusts. But this business with her mother keeps getting in the way.

Jem has been quiet since we met up after school. She didn't buy any lunch and I'm worried that she was going to make herself ill as I watch her push fishfingers, peas and potato wedges around her plate. She looks a little depressed, I think I would be in her position. Even when I'd said, "See you in the morning", she'd just nodded in response.

After Jem leaves, I ask Gran what she thinks of Jem's situation. I know she is worried about her too.

"I don't know what we're going to do, Noah, but something needs to be done. A friend of mine knows a bit about domestic violence in the home. I could try to foster her but I need to look into it. There's a lot of red tape and I can't see Joyce letting her stay here with me. She likes having Jemima to do her skivvying and gets a lot of enjoyment from treating her with such contempt. Let's sleep on it."

I nod and head home. Tomorrow, we'll think of something.

At home I help Mum with any chores before Dad comes home from work, and then head to my room to make a start on my homework. After about an hour I get sidetracked as I google "Domestic Violence". I look at the links and am shocked by the statistics and facts. No one wants to think of themselves as a weak person or a victim, but this type of abuse is instigated by someone who is supposed to love and care for you. Someone who builds a sense of power. Someone who gets off on holding power over you and uses violence to berate, belittle, punish and control. It's shocking. I close my eyes and try to block it out.

I must have fallen asleep because the sun is streaming through the curtains when I wake. I stare at my alarm clock. Jesus it's 8am. I need to get up.

I jump out of bed, grab some clothes and start dressing. I pick up my bag and mobile, quickly grab some toast and juice and head to Jem's house. If I run I can make it there in five minutes. The first thing I notice is that her bedroom curtains are still drawn. A shiver rushes down my spine as I push the buzzer to the front door. No answer. I press again.

The door is pulled open and Joyce stands there.

"Where is she?" I ask

"Upstairs. The lazy cow hasn't got up yet."

Something just doesn't feel right. A tall, bald guy pushes past me.

"I'm late…" He says without looking at Joyce. He pushes the key fob to his car as she follows him.

"Pete, see you tonight then?"

"Maybe," he mutters. "I think I'm busy, but I'll text you."

"Peeete," she whines.

"For Christ's sake…leave me alone, woman!" He sneers at her, gets into his car and drives off.

I take this opportunity to go and find Jemima. That feeling that something isn't quite right keeps building and I'm not sure what I'll find when I get to her room.

"Jem!" I call.

"Lazy cow!" Joyce shouts upstairs.

Then, finally, as I push the door to her bedroom open I find what I've been dreading. Well not quite as bad as I've been dreading. I thought that maybe her mother had hurt her badly and she was bedridden or worse. I stare around the room, looking at her things, looking for a clue as to where she might be. Where could she have gone? She's only fifteen for Christ's sake.

Absently I pick up one of her discarded doodle books and flick through. My eye catches on a page which has a small sketch of someone who looks very much like me. He is looking up at something, his eyes focusing and lips smiling at someone who may be standing above him. She drew me...I'm sort of shocked. I'm also sort of pleased that she thought of me. I spy another notebook and tuck both in my jacket pocket. Somehow they make me feel close to her.

I wish I knew what had happened to her. Wish I had talked to her yesterday and told her how I feel. Instead, I look at the empty room and slowly my world folds in on itself.

Chapter 7:
The Lighthouse: now (Jem)

There is one simple rule to abide by when you become involved in the refuge facilities that Jenny Greyson and her husband, Stuart, have spent their lives building and maintaining. The Lighthouse is a charity run family organisation that is defined by its code of conduct and rules. The charity's aim and ethos are based on being able to offer a place of safety and solace for women and children who are in danger. A place where new lives can eventually be re-shaped with newly built confidence. People who have faith in the inner strength of a soul and an understanding that the power to move forward, with the right support, opportunities and love, is within a person.

There is one rule that overshadows everything else. That rule is that we keep the confidentiality of information and whereabouts of all those who live and work there. The safety of the vulnerable, whether adult or child, is paramount. In simple layman's terms, Jenny and Stuart Greyson saved my life.

I overslept. I was planning to be up and ready with the coffee, but I'd slept so well it was the first time in a long time when I hadn't felt as though I'd had a night of uninterrupted sleep. I woke with a start, glared at the alarm clock and realised it was 8.45am. I quickly dressed and headed to the bathroom to freshen up and make myself presentable. I put some toothpaste on my finger, added some water and rubbed it quickly across my teeth, hoping to get rid of that sour taste in my mouth. I made a mental note to buy myself a new toothbrush.

Jenny was sitting at the kitchen table with Maureen. Her long blonde hair still reached her shoulders as I remembered, and her frame was still tall and slim. With very graceful movements she reached to pull apart a *pain au chocolat* and pop it into her mouth.

"Jenny." My voice sounded odd, as if I was fifteen again and needed someone to protect me and help keep me safe.

"Hey, sweetie," she says standing up and walking toward me with her arms open. "How are you doing?"

"I'm okay," I say walking into her hug. "Just need to lay low for a while and get my head sorted," I said holding her tight, as years of memories swam around my head and took hold of my heart. The emotion of those vulnerable years spent in one of The Lighthouse homes; keeping me safe, fed, loved, schooled and pushing me to be something more, to wanting more out of life, was almost too much for me. This woman helped me to develop the confidence in myself and to reach out and make my life a success. To say I was a little overcome with emotion as I tried to hold in the tears was an understatement.

"Joyce?" She addressed the elephant in the room which immediately pulled me back to reality.

"Yes. She turned up out of the blue at my wedding. I think there was a connection between Craig and Joyce. Not sure how they met but I plan to find out why and what they are up to."

The back door opened and in walked Noah as though he lived here. I hadn't expected to see him today. Don't get me wrong, I was secretly pleased that he was here for me, but there were things that I needed to say to Jenny and I was worried about the "Rule".

"Sorry I'm late," he said jovially and nodded to everyone in turn.

"This is Noah, my grandson," said Maureen looking at Jenny.

Jenny acknowledges him with a careful smile and looks at me. "You okay with Noah being here?"

I look at Noah, he deserves to be part of this now. He had always been there for me when I was a child and deserved to be involved in this new chapter of my life. A life that was quickly becoming more complicated by the minute, and which included the fledgling relationship now developing between myself and Noah.

I need him to know about my life, about my painting and about Craig. It's important for us to do this if we want to move forward and I'd prefer to move forward with him rather than without him. I couldn't wait to fill in the blanks with his life too. *Slow down*, *Jem*, I tell myself. I need to stay focused and work through this business with my mother and Craig first.

"Yes," answers Jenny. I move to the kitchen table and help myself to a pastry. Stuffing the delicious *pain au raisin* partly into my mouth, I savour the taste that brings back old memories of early morning work meetings with newly formed friends in a small coffee shop in Lyme Regis. I swallow and head to the kettle. "But I need a coffee before we start."

Noah takes the kettle from me and fills it up.

"Anyone else?" Maureen and Jenny point to their mugs and shake their heads.

"I take my coffee black. For future reference." He smiles at me.

"White with one sugar. Coffee or tea. For future reference," I inform him as I finish making my coffee and taking a quick slurp.

We sit down at the table. This was going to be hard. But it needed to be done.

"Okay. So, I'll start at the beginning. Jenny, you know most of this, but I'll recap for Maureen and Noah. I met Craig about a year ago. He came into the coffee shop when I was reading my Kindle one day. We started chatting. He made the first move. Thinking back, it was always Craig making the first move. Was the coffee meeting pre-arranged? I don't know. I caught him snooping in my house and he found my paints and easels in the spare bedroom. I think he suspected something."

Maureen and Noah looked at each other. I guess it was time to share some important information.

"Remember when I used to doodle a lot? Well, it's a long story of which I'll happily fill you in at some point, but for now – all you need to know is that I met someone who saw my drawings and paintings and happened to be an agent. Chloe signed me up and I have had some success with my paintings."

Maureen looked at Noah. He said nothing, just looked back at Maureen.

"You are an artist and you make a living from it?" Maureen asks.

"Yes, and she's pretty successful too," Jenny says with some pride.

"Hold on a minute." Maureen stops, holding her hands up. "But your mother, how did you hide from her? You're successful? I don't think I've seen your work, have I?"

"She doesn't use her real name," Noah announces quietly. His eyes bore into mine as if suddenly realising the only way to avoid detection is to create a persona that leaves my real identity a secret.

"Yes, you're right," I admit, feeling a little unsure of how this will make me look to these people who I used to be so close to. Using an alias wasn't really a lie, just a creative way to move forward so that I could paint and become self-sufficient.

"Marnie Lake," Noah states.

We all stare at Noah. How the bloody hell does he know that? Maureen raises her eyebrows in shock. Jenny looks suspicious, clearly unsure what to make of Noah and his correct assumption.

"How did you know?" I asked him. I couldn't look him in the eye.

"Something about Marnie's style that reminded me of you and your earlier drawings. The brush strokes, the stark theme sometimes. I've got several pieces myself at home."

"You have? Oh my god! Noah! I'm speechless…I don't know what to say." That's a first for me. I was desperate to ask what pieces of my work he had, why he liked them and where he'd put them in the house. I was desperate to understand how Noah could recognise something from the paintings that reminded him of me.

"Sorry to bring you back to reality but we need to discuss your mother, Joyce." Jenny's voice interrupts my thoughts and I realise that hard as it is, we do need to focus on the current problem.

"Craig said he thought I should have at least one member of my family at the wedding. I told him no. I made it clear that I was not in touch with what little family I had left and that my reasons were my own. I insinuated that there was some bad history between us. This was about a month ago. He never mentioned it again."

"When I walked down the aisle at the register office, the first thing I saw was her, at the back, wearing a beige suit and brown floppy hat. I took two steps before the realisation that I wasn't dreaming set in. I hadn't seen her for ten years. That woman had the audacity to smile at me and say 'Congratulations darling' as I walked past her. I saw Craig's sheepish face staring back at me. Liar. How could he? What right had he to get involved in my business? As his family looked on, including his smiling parents and some of our friends, all I could think about was that he had purposely got in touch with her and instigated her attendance at the wedding.

"I was about four feet from him and fuming. Then I started to scream at him while still clutching my red and white roses in my hands, and before I knew it I'd hurled them at him and stormed out. I didn't stop until I got to my car."

Noah puts his hand on top of mine and strokes my knuckles softly. Is this weird or what? I mean, here I am telling him about how I was about to marry someone else and he's stroking my hand.

The phone rings and Maureen stands and moves to the cupboard to answer it. She looks first at me and then at Jenny.

It's her, she mouths. Jesus, that was quick.

Jenny looks at me. She knows me well enough to understand that I need to confront my mother and that I cannot keep running. The Lighthouse would always be there to support me, but now I am an adult things are different. Circumstances have changed. Now I have property, funds and friends to support me.

The running is over.

"Tell her I'm here," I say to Maureen.

"If she touches so much as a hair on your head I am going to fucking kill her," Noah says, more to himself than to me.

Jenny listens and seems happy to see how protective Noah is of me. Maureen puts the phone down and heads back to the table.

"Well, she's on her way. And she's bringing Craig."

"Oh great. Craig and more lies."

"Don't worry," Jenny says. "We've got this. We're here for you. You won't be left on your own with either of them. I'll update Stuart and we'll both be on standby. I know the answer already, but just to make sure, do you want to stay at one of the homes?"

I look at Noah, the strength he gives me bolsters me.

"No more running. I'm going to stay here. She's back for something and I am going to find out what."

For now I also need my basic things, such as a mobile, laptop, clothes and access to money. It's funny how you can never remember phone numbers because you always use mobiles, names and speed dial…

"Maureen, are you okay if I make a couple of calls? Noah, can you google the number for Chloe Green, her company is called Impressions Artists. Thanks. I need to call Chloe so that she can get my emergency stuff ready. I'll need to start using my other bank card and account and cancel the other. I was in such a rush to get away I left everything in the hotel room where I changed into my wedding dress and where we were supposed to spend the night. Chloe was at the ceremony, so she may have already sorted that for me. She knew about mother so she will have an idea why I ran."

Noah wrote down the phone number for Chloe's agency and put the paper in my hand.

Jenny looks at me thoughtfully.

"If Joyce is aware of the money, or she and Craig are aware, that could be motive for setting you up to be married. Once married to him, he could discredit you or something equally dire and recommend that he could keep the money in trust for you."

The money. Another red warning flag panics me and tries to threaten my new life. I'm not good at sharing information. After all, I've spent my entire life being cautious and watching over my shoulder.

Noah and Maureen look at me.

"My paintings are really successful," I explain. "I still have to pinch myself to believe that people want to pay for my work. I used to sketch and paint the lamp-post from outside of this house. I developed a series of paintings depicting various seasons, and for some reason a famous rock star bought the whole lot for an obscene amount of money! That was the beginning."

"Are you a millionaire?" Noah asks.

"Yes, and some. Though I don't feel or live like one."

"She's being very modest," Jenny says. "She is also a silent partner in The Lighthouse charity and regularly contributes to funds and board meetings. In fact, Stuart and I could not achieve as much for the charity without Jem's input."

"Oh my goodness, Jem." Maureen puts her arm around me. "I'm so proud of you and what you've achieved." I smile up at her and feel grateful that she still feels this way about me even after all this time. I am still the same person that she used to know, still like the same things such as sticky toffee pudding, still doodle things that catch my eye until my fingers ache, and still feel that strong bond between her, Noah and myself.

Noah sits quietly with an unhappy look on his face and I study his features to gauge his thoughts. It would appear that he doesn't feel quite as proud of me as Maureen does. No hugs are offered or kind words to say well done. I suddenly feel deflated.

"Noah?"

"Jem, I'm not sure why I'm caught out by this, but I just need a minute to get my head around it all. You're an artist, a famous artist, and you're also a millionaire at least. So much to take in, you know. As of yesterday I hadn't seen you for the past ten years."

"I know," I say sadly. "Take your time."

Jenny stands, throwing her bag over her shoulder.

"For now, I need to go home and speak to Stuart. I'll get Jack, our new investigator, to check out your mother and her finances. She's the sort who can't keep out of trouble, so if she's heading this way we should at least have an idea of why. You remember Jack was at the wedding with Chloe yesterday, right? He saw what happened and took her to your room to get your things before your mother or Craig got hold of them. If you sort things with Chloe, I'll be back with Stuart tonight after seven, unless I hear from you before." She makes for the door.

"Thank God Jack was there. I forgot about that! I know we agreed to keep my painter alias and my real name a secret for now, so I told Craig that I worked at the art gallery with Chloe and Jack. I would have told him soon after we married though. Didn't want to start our marriage with too many secrets." I mutter the last bit more to myself.

Noah stands up. "I need a bit of fresh air. I'll walk you to the door." He walks behind Jenny as she says her goodbyes.

Maureen puts her arm around my shoulder as I watch them both leave.

"Don't worry about Noah, he's got a few things on his mind. He had to grow up fast after his parents went, but he's used to being organised and in control. He's got his own business, plus Suzanne, and then there's your arrival too. Oh dear, it will all come together in the end I'm sure."

"What did you say about his parents?" I ask, and my heart suddenly misses a beat with the news that Noah's parents were no longer with us. His parents were lovely people and a pang of sadness hits me. My first thought is to ask Maureen what happened, but I hold my tongue.

"I shouldn't have said anything. That's his story to tell you and I'm sure he will when he feels the time is right. I lost my daughter too. You never get over your child dying before you." A tear slips down her cheek. Goodness, how much this woman has suffered, and, I bet, still suffers. I stare at her and move forward.

"I'm so sorry, Maureen," I say hugging her as tightly as I can. "I don't want my visit here to cause you problems and make you unhappy."

I hope that Noah will tell me what happened with his parents in his own way and own time.

"You won't, lass. This is not your fault."

Noah comes back in looking somewhat brighter in demeanour. Well, at least not looking at me as though I'm his least favourite person to be around. He comes to stand in front of me and starts speaking.

"Call Chloe, let's get your things sorted out first. Then I'm taking you out for a few hours. We need to talk."

I look at him, take in that "I'm not taking no for an answer" tone in his voice and the set look on his face. I was too used to looking after myself, relying wholly on myself to get things done, so it was hard giving up the reins and giving someone else control. But deep down I felt weary and a little broken. Without saying another word, I pick up the paper with Chloe's details on and head for the phone.

Chapter 8:
Starting over: then (Jem)

I've lost track of time. My head leans limply against the passenger car window. Jenny is driving. She knows that I want to keep quiet and doesn't make any attempt at conversation. I keep going over my last moments with Maureen as she hugs me, nearly crunching my ribs. I can still feel her shaking with sobs and trying bravely to hold them as we said goodbye.

"This is for the best," Maureen says softly as we hug. "You will be safe away from your mother and this will give you that much needed and deserved chance to start over."

"I know," I nod, but tears are running down my cheeks. "But what will you tell Noah? I don't want to leave like this."

"Now, look here, young lady. When you arrived here tonight you were ready to head out on your own, catch whatever bus and whatever train to go to god knows where. You have a real chance to be safe to live a life without wondering if you will be alive tomorrow or concussed or whatever that woman who has no right to call herself your mother may have done to you. I feel happier knowing that Jenny is looking out for you from now on. Noah will think that you've run away. One day he may find out the truth, but for now – this needs to be about you. This is your time. Don't look back."

"I love you, Maureen."

"You too, sweetie." I'd given her one last squeeze, grabbed my bag and headed out into the darkness with Jenny. She opens the passenger door of her car and motions for me to get inside. I do so with a heavy heart. I smile weakly at Maureen and give a half-hearted wave. A wave of silent pleas fill my head as Jenny starts the car. *Please let it be okay, please let it be the right thing to do. Please let Noah forgive me for this.* The car starts moving and I stare at the window.

"It will be okay." Jenny's voice breaks into my thoughts.

I look at her outline in the dark. Our eyes meet and I nod. It's all I can manage.

I think I may have nodded off in the car because a soft voice and gentle hand pulls me out of my slumber.

"Jemima, we're here."

"It's Jem. Noah and my school friends call me Jem."

"Thanks for letting me know that. It's good to start on the right foot. Well, Jem, we're here."

In the darkness I realise that we have driven into a gated driveway. The gate is now beginning to close and we seem secure away from the outside world. There is a detached Victorian house that looks like something out of a gothic novel and light reflects through the part drawn curtains of the lower floor windows. The front door opens, and standing there with the confidence of someone who has done this before stands a tall man with short mousy hair.

"Jemima, welcome. I'm Stuart."

"It's Jem," Jenny states nodding slowly at me.

"Welcome, Jem. Come along. I've got the kettle on and biscuits on hand. We'll explain what happens from here."

It suddenly seemed strange to be thinking of tea and biscuits in the early hours of the morning. I checked my watch. It was 1.30am. God, where was I? Was I really going to go through with this?

I follow Stuart in through the main door still carrying my bag on my back and find myself in a state-of-the-art kitchen. I sit at the dining table as Jenny switches on the kettle.

When the hot steaming mugs of tea are placed on the table and the adults are sitting in front of me, I take out my phone and lay it on the table beside my mug. Stuart speaks first.

"Jem, we want to help you. Jenny and I manage two refuge centres – we call them homes – for those needing protection and support. Usually we have a mum and child or children to place and usually we get referrals from outside agencies and councils. Your situation is very unusual."

"However," Jenny carries on, "we do have a place for you to stay. We also have contacts with a high school near the home so that you can continue your education."

"That's good." I take a deep breath feeling both relief and panic. I know I have no choice. If I don't go what choice do I have? Get on a bus or train to somewhere unknown hoping to find somewhere safe to live, or take a huge leap of faith with these people.

"And quick," I add. "I guess the question is where is it I need to go?"

"Lyme Regis. West Dorset. How do you feel about that?"

"For a chance at a future life without pain or threats, a move to Lyme Regis sounds good, really good."

"Great. That's what we wanted to hear. Our job is always hard, dealing with emotions and broken families. Knowing that you understand what we are trying to do and how we are trying to keep you safe and cared for is a huge step in the right direction."

Stuart picks up his mobile and puts together a text, then presses send. "So, we'll finish off here and get some sleep upstairs. There's a spare bedroom up there for you, Jem. Don't rush to get up in the morning. We'll have breakfast when you're ready and aim to get to Lyme between 11 and 12 noon tomorrow. Is that okay with you?"

I nod my head. "Yes, I feel like I could sleep forever."

"We'll need to throw your phone away. I'll have a new one sent to the Lyme home tomorrow for you. That way no one can contact you, and please don't get the temptation to contact anyone from your past. We need to make sure that your mother has no access to you. We can discuss further options in the coming weeks."

I look at Jenny and Stuart in turn. These people who hadn't met me until three hours ago, who had collected me from Maureen's and made me feel welcome in their home, and who are willing to protect me until I am old enough to look after myself. Somewhere out there must be my guardian angel sending these people to me. All at once everything became too much and I burst into tears. A swift movement catches the corner of my eye as Jenny pulls back her chair, stoops down and puts her arm around me.

She holds me tight, whispering over and over, "It will be okay, it will be okay." Cautiously I slide my arms around her until I feel myself relax. I take a deep breath and for no reason other than she is here, I hold on tight.

"Let's get you to bed. Some rest will make all the difference." She leads me upstairs and shows me to a lovely pastel painted room with a double bed and an adjoining bathroom. She then shows me to the bathroom and demonstrates how to open the window that happens to be a little stiff and then leaves me. I quickly use the bathroom, find my PJs and am asleep as soon as my head hits the pillow.

The first thing that hits me when I wake the following morning is the smell of bacon cooking somewhere within the house. Delicious! My first thought is to rush downstairs to help prepare breakfast, but then I remember that Mother is not in the house.

This whole situation feels really weird and I feel slightly disorientated about this unfamiliar environment. I have never woken into a house where there was no shouting or banging. This will take some getting used to.

I shower, dress, shove my mobile in my jeans pocket and head downstairs. I follow the sound of low voices, which I think are coming from the kitchen area. I hadn't noticed much of the house last night, or should I say this morning, as I had been so tired and dazed and the house was mostly in darkness.

There are clean cream walls everywhere from the hallway to the lounge, but with accents of dark mahogany furniture and blasts of colourful artwork dotted around feature walls. The kitchen, however, has a bright yellow feature wall against white shiny units and dark worktops. Very modern. Very welcoming and bright. *Not something I have ever experienced at home,* I suddenly think with a pang.

"Good morning, Jem." Jenny comes over to me, smiling warmly, and gives me a reassuring shoulder hug.

"Morning," I replied.

"You hungry?" Stuart asks, pointing to the pile of bacon and eggs he is building on the hotplate.

I don't think my stomach can digest any food with everything that's going on, but the growing plate of food begins to slowly awaken my taste buds.

I nod appreciatively, after all he's gone to a lot of trouble.

"That looks good." I point to the growing plate. "Are you expecting visitors?" I ask cautiously.

"No. But Jenny and I have got big appetites and we were hoping you were the same!" he says with a cheeky grin.

Jenny goes to a cupboard, turns, and motions for me to sit down at the dining table. I sit waiting for them both to join me and watch Jenny carefully as she puts mugs and a pot of tea alongside the sugar bowl and milk jug on the table. Stuart brings the food across to the table and tells us to help ourselves. Finally, when they are both sitting, I look at the glorious array of food in front of me and can't help but feel that it's the last supper.

As I peck at my food my mobile bleeps. It's the first time that I've checked it since leaving Maureen's. There are several texts from Noah asking where I am. They start off casually and slowly become more desperate and panic ridden. Bloody hell! This is hard. My first urge is to text him back, but I know I can't.

"It's my friend Noah. He's looking for me," I say in a way of explanation as my eyes keep wandering back to my phone.

Stuart looks at Jenny and then nods to my phone.

"You know you can text him. However, I would advise strongly against giving him your whereabouts. We need to get you settled into the Lyme home first then we can reassess your contact with your old life and if that's possible. To be honest, we don't know for sure that it's Noah sending those texts. In our experience a new start basically means a new start."

I nod feeling a little hollow as I leave Noah's texts unanswered. Stuart's right. I need to let go, it's the only way. Perhaps later when I'm sorted...

Jenny puts her hand over mine.

"We're here for you. You'll be fine. We'll go through every step of the way with you. Try not to worry too much."

Right now I wish I had someone familiar to turn to such as Maureen or Noah. My old life feels closed off and a new future is being planned for me. I need to believe that this is for the best and that I deserve this new beginning.

"Let's get your things together and we'll start the drive to Lyme."

I look at my half-empty plate. The need for food seems to have left me. I pour the last of the warm tea down my throat and head upstairs to collect my things.

The drive to Lyme seems to take forever. I'm sitting on my own in the back of the car. I've got my pencils and doodle pad and I am lazily drawing an image of Noah and Maureen. I know I won't forget them but seeing their familiar faces on my book seems to give me some comfort.

Finally, we reach a pretty detached house not far from the bay and near the centre of town. Jenny reassures me with a smile. There are vibrant purple flowers in pots on either side of the front door. The door is painted white, as are the pots. It looks nice.

Someone opens the front door and steps towards us.

"Hello, Jem. Welcome to Shore House. I'm Lottie and this will be your new home."

"Hey, Lottie," I try hard to be brave. "Thank you for having me."

The grown-ups exchange brief hugs and Jenny takes my hand.

"Come on, Jem. Let's show you around. It's a great place to live."

Jenny seems so excited as she shows me around. I know I will get used to the various rooms, but right now this place feels a little like the Tardis. The decor is clean and simple. Pale light colours bring a calmness to the home and the furniture looks well cared for and expensive as dark mahogany bookshelves, cupboards and a dining table adorn the rooms. Clearly someone has spent a lot of money to ensure that this place is a very welcoming environment.

One day I would love to repay Stuart and Jenny back for their kindness, help and support. I make a silent promise to myself that if I were ever able to, I would give back to this charity, whether offering money, actions or time. Anything I could do to support the future of the homes to enable vulnerable children and people to have a safe-haven, would become one of my lifetime passions.

Lottie motions for us all to sit and disappears to pop the kettle on. A tall woman with long dark curly hair and wearing a shoulder support for what looks like a plastered broken arm comes into the room. Hiding behind her is a little boy. He's maybe three or four years old.

"Hi. It's Jem, right? I'm Steph," she smiles. "And this little scamp is Ben. He's three. Come and say hello to Jem, Ben."

The cutie pops out from his mum's longline jumper. He wiggles with excitement and jumps into a sort of star shape, saying loudly, "Hi, I'm Ben! Look, I can jump really high." Ben, with a determined look on his face, proceeds to jump several times as high as he possibly can and eventually almost knocks the side table over.

"Careful, Ben, you're not Superman you know," Steph warns her little man as Ben looks up at her, smiling sweetly.

"Yeth, I am."

Lottie returns with a tray of tea and biscuits. She pours drinks for everyone and finally says, "Welcome to Shore House, Jem."

I take in everyone's smiles and nods and think that this place is just what I need. I think that I might like living here.

Shore House is my new beginning.

Chapter 9:
Clearing the air: now (Jem)

Well, this isn't where I thought I'd be yesterday! I sink into the plush seat and comfort of Noah's Audi Q7, my hands are clamped together on my lap to stop myself from shaking. Noah drives swiftly through the lanes and heads out onto the coastal road. I don't know where we're going, and he hasn't said a word to me since I got in the car. I'd told Maureen to call Noah if my mother and Craig turned up. Hopefully, my stuff including my phone are being courier delivered to Maureen at some point this afternoon.

We pull into the car park at a local beauty spot and Noah turns off the engine. He turns to me and starts speaking.

"When you first left I used to come here a lot."

I didn't know what to say. So, in my infinite wisdom, I say nothing.

"I took your notebooks from your room and used to sit on the beach, look out to sea and simply hold them – to feel close to you."

A tear falls down my cheek and he leans forward to wipe it away with his thumb.

"Let's go for a walk."

I follow his lead as we leave the car behind and start to walk along the sand. I'm wearing an old jacket that belongs to

Maureen. It's padded and warm and my hands are stuffed in the side pockets.

"My parents died five years ago in a car crash. Did Maureen tell you?"

I wasn't expecting that. I look at him suddenly. He's wearing a zip up hoodie with the hood down and T-shirt underneath and some faded black jeans. He is older, we both are, and we are different people now, but there's something between us that keeps us tied together. There's a sense of understanding, like a pair of old souls with a powerful feeling of connection to each other. I have never felt this with Craig.

"Yes. She mentioned it. I'm so sorry."

"They thought the world of you, you know. Couldn't understand how that bitch mother of yours could produce someone as lovely as you."

"Noah." I really needed a hug from him right now. But with my little world in such turmoil and my emotions shot, I just couldn't bring myself to touch him for fear of rejection.

"Jem, there are things that I should tell you about...about me, about Suzanne. But first, there is something that I really need to do."

Without warning, Noah turns to face me and takes me in his arms. His hands scoop my face, bringing it up to meet his, and he kisses me as though the world is about to end. We've never really kissed before unless you count that quick touch of the lips in Maureen's house yesterday. This is nothing like that. It is everything I'd hoped it would be, like the best chocolate dessert in the world that leaves you feeling satisfied but wanting more.

My arms slide up to his neck as my fingers explore his skin and hair. So, this is what it's like in the movies. Those moments of romantic bliss that you think are overacted to look more passionate for the camera. My heart melts and a feeling of bliss overwhelms me and stirs my senses. Such an immense sense of peace envelopes me, and it feels as though I've arrived home.

Noah pulls away gently, his eyes show a brightness as if he's found the answer to a long-lost secret, before he nods to a nearby bench. Without thinking I take his hand and he quickly threads his fingers through mine. We smile like intoxicated teenagers. This is a big thing for us, a game changer.

When we're sitting we both stare as the waves come in onto the sand.

"I found your notebooks after you left…I found those drawings of me," he says still looking out to sea.

"I loved catching those moments when you were lost in thought. It made me feel closer to you."

"Did you ever think of me over the years?"

"Yes, often. Did you think of me?" I ask, desperately hoping that he'll say yes.

"What do you think, Jem? Of course I bloody thought of you! Even though I had no idea if you were dead or alive!"

Anger mixes with honesty and I put my hand on his thigh to calm him. I try to put myself in his place. If Noah had been the one to leave without a note or warning, I think I would have driven myself insane trying to find him or trying to find out what had happened to him.

Noah puts his hand on top of mine. I feel that there's something that he wants to tell me, that he's building up to, and I just wish he would spit it out and say it.

"So, you know when I said we needed to talk?" he begins.

"Yes," I answer.

"Over the years a lot of things have happened to both of us. You are a famous painter, you have an alias and money. God, that took a while to get my head around. But I remember what a talented artist you were – even at fifteen – and I knew deep down that if you were still alive that you would have done well for yourself. I'm so proud of you, Jem. So, so proud." He takes his hand from my thigh and draws me to him in a big, possessive hug.

"Tell me about Suzanne?" Maybe this isn't the best time to bring it up but it's like the elephant in the room, and I need to know if my feelings should be held in check because of a relationship he is having with someone else.

"She's my business partner and girlfriend. I passed my law degree, got as much legal experience as I could and started a small law firm in Weymouth a couple of years ago. I met Suzanne last year and we started dating five months ago. She's great. Kind, strong, beautiful and clever."

I feel my heart sinking. I stiffen, but his arm stays firm around my shoulder.

"And in I walk like a ghost from the past and stirring up old memories. I'm sorry, Noah. So sorry."

I feel like I'm forever saying this lately. My energy levels drop drastically as I try desperately not to let this news upset me. I can't afford to become despondent when I have my mother to face. I know I have no right to expect anything from Noah. Ten years holds a lot of history, experiences and feelings for both of us. I know I did the right thing moving away when I was fifteen, but hell, sometimes, just sometimes, I wonder what would have happened if I'd stayed.

His mobile buzzed. He withdraws his arm to take out his phone and looks at the caller sign. He quickly reads the text.

"It's Gran. Your mother and Craig have arrived."

"My mother still has crap timing," I mutter, and start to make my way back to the car.

"Hey, wait." He pulls me around so I'm facing him.

"We'll work this out," he says quietly. "Let's take it one day at a time."

This is just what I wanted to hear. What I needed to hear.

"Come, let's go face that bitch of a mother and the ditched groom. Jesus, if someone saw me now they'd think I was on a reality TV show!" He strides forward, shaking his head.

Yes. That's my life. A reality TV show where anything goes, people play up to the camera, inadvertently showing their true colours. Throw in a dose of no rules or boundaries and some good people trying to watch your back, yes – a perfect storm of reality. Let's see what games we will be playing today. *Please give me the strength to cope with my mother so that I can find out what she is up to,* I think to myself.

We are both quiet on the drive back to Maureen's. Both deep in thought about our circumstances and what we will find. There is also the uncertainty of our future either together or apart. As Noah parks the car he turns to me and brushes my cheek softly with his hand.

"Tell me something. Craig, do you still love him?" he asks, not taking his eyes from mine.

"No," I say honestly. "I don't think I ever really did, I just wanted the dream."

"And Suzanne?"

"I was beginning to feel that she was the one. But now you're back I realise that I was holding on for something more. For you."

I put my hand to his cheek and he leans in. This is going to be tough, but I can see the light at the end of the tunnel. A small glimmer of hope begins to build within me for a life that I've dreamed of since being a little girl. I want the fairy tale.

We get out of the car and head to the front door.

"Let's get this over with," he says as the front door is yanked open by Maureen. Stuart and Jenny stand behind her and I can hear the cackle of my mother's voice in the background. "Here's my darling girl."

My first thought is: Shit! She knows about the money. Let the games begin.

Chapter 10:
Time to move on: five years ago (Noah)

The beat of the music is booming through my headphones. No matter how high I turn up Bruce Springsteen, the constant banging and shouting can still be heard. Jesus, when will they go to bed? I check my watch again. It's 1.30pm. I've got an assignment that needs to be finished in forty-eight hours and a couple of my 'Halls' flat room mates are plaguing me with their constant partying. They're in the kitchen area, drinking with invited friends, and the drink is making them louder by the minute.

Generally they're a good bunch, three boys and two girls, including myself share this five-bedroomed flat, all enjoying the first flush of freedom and independence in the Halls residence complex. I cannot believe that at almost twenty-one years of age I'm sitting here pushing myself with everything I've got to try to give myself a better future. I'm the first person to want a drink, but I know that getting this final assignment that almost completes my first year done is crucial.

Bruce screams out "Thunder Road" and I try to concentrate on finishing a paragraph which I've been stuck on for the last five minutes. I miss the knock at the door. The first time I notice that I'm not alone is when I feel a hand on my shoulder. I take off the headphones and look at Bella who is on my course. I take in the long blue T-shirt that drops to the top of her thighs. She looks kind of cute in her nightshirt, reminding me of that old rhyme about what little girls are made of.

"Can't get any work done." She looks at me as though I have a magic wand and can put an end to the noise and disruption so that we can sleep or carry on with our assignments.

"Me neither," I say, watching warily as she sits on my bed and crosses her legs.

"Do you want to chill together for a while?" she says, stroking her fingers along the stripes on my duvet cover. Bella is a lovely girl. Her short, dark curly hair reminds me a little of Jem. Suddenly my heart skips a beat at the thought of her. Where is she? What was she doing? Was she alive or dead? I haven't thought of Jem in a while now. I've kept myself busy with studies and haven't had much interest in girls. Was I secretly hoping that Jem would come back? Because I'm now pretty sure after five long years that she won't.

Perhaps it's time to move on. I'm young, I'm free and I'm single, so maybe I should stop acting like someone who has been through too much and start living some of this life I've been given. I don't want to look back with too many regrets. I need to find a way to enjoy life again, to forget the past, enjoy the present and focus on the future.

I put my headphones on my desk, save the work I am working on and put my mobile on silent. I look at Bella, she's sitting waiting patiently for my response.

"Sure. What did you have in mind?" I say, sitting down next to her and smiling with as much confidence as I can muster.

"Do you fancy a nightcap?" she asks with a smile. I lean in to stroke her face. I'm looking for a signal to say that she's okay with this. She nods as her hands slowly wind their way up my back to my neck, slowly stroking my skin. I move in to give her a quick kiss and suddenly feel the pull of emotion that has been stamped down within me for the past few years. The kiss lasts forever.

I'd forgotten what it was like to be close to someone. I'd missed the touch of another person and I'd missed the connection that being close to someone brings. The last person I was touchy feely close to was Jem. This feels a bit like a betrayal of her, but I need to push myself if I want a chance of moving forward.

"I've got some beers in the fridge in the kitchen," I say to Bella. "I'll be back in a minute."

The sun shining through the curtains wakes me and thoughts of Bella and our time together before she went back to her room come flooding back to me. I smile to myself as I remembered how we sat talking and kissing until it was time to get some sleep. She was an enjoyable distraction with her soft kisses and smiles. The thought leaves me feeling happier inside than I've felt in a long while.

I check my mobile. Shit. I remember that I'd turned it on silent.

There are several missed calls and texts from Gran.

Call me urgently. Need to talk to you, they read.

I looked at the clock. It was 8am. I call her.

I speak to Gran who is crying into the phone. She's half mumbling through tears and hiccups which makes her a little hard to understand. Eventually, she gets around to saying what she's been trying to say since hearing my voice at the other end of the phone. My parents have been killed in a car crash on the motorway, coming home from an IKEA shopping trip.

Fuck! Gran tells me that she's taking the first train to come and get me just before I put the phone down.

So much for moving forward. I can't think, can't say anything, can't move.

My parents are dead, and my life will change forever.

Chapter 11:
A Picasso in the making: five years ago (Jem)

I love living at Shore House. There is always something going on and I mean that in a good way. Jenny and Stuart come to visit me every weekend to see how I'm doing and they're happy for me to call them anytime I need help or to talk. Sometimes we go off for the day at the weekend, museums, walks, festivals. I like going to the beach best.

My doodle pads are no longer small notebooks but real sketch pads now and I often find myself engrossed in a moment of sheer bliss and concentration. The world has so many beautiful things in it. I love watching the people, their expressions, love, hate, surprise.

Natural elements such as the waves on the sea, curves in landscape or a building have also captured my interest over the years. Inanimate objects such as the lamp-post that I would watch when I used to visit Maureen. Guess what? There's a lamp-post on the opposite pavement of Shore House that I can see from my bedroom window! How cool is that? I love watching and sketching the different shades and contours as the light changes throughout the day. I've tried working with oil paints and watercolours. I prefer watercolours.

I've just started my final end of year art college project working on a set of four paintings of the lamp-posts in soft watercolours that depict the changing seasons. The way the light fuses from the shade to the pavement in clean sweeps intrigues the artist in me. The paintings will be showcased in an art gallery evening being shown at the college in three weeks. As you can imagine, everyone in class is panicking about their project and hoping theirs will be finished on time. I'm no different. I've still got two paintings to do. Our lecturer, Eric, has invited a wide range of artists, agents and local buyers to the event, so there's no pressure at all!

Lottie reminds me so much of Maureen, always checking in but giving me space. She has that light touch when she walks past me, whether I'm sitting at the dining table catching up on college work for my art and design diploma or heading out of the door. Lottie isn't afraid to give hugs and offers praise without consequences, both natural characteristics one might find in a good friend or even a mother figure. I will always be grateful for having her, Jenny and Stuart in my life.

I often think of Maureen and Noah and wonder if they are okay. I will grudgingly admit to stalking Noah on Facebook to see what he is doing. What a sad soul am I! Can you believe that he's training to be a solicitor at university? He's a little older than me, although we were in the same year at school. His Facebook photos show how much he's changed. He's no longer a boy. God help any girls he meets. He'll chew them up for dinner! He's got this sort of no-nonsense, rugged look about him that makes me feel drawn to him, protective of him and attracted to him all at the same time.

I cannot believe that I have been here for five years and that I am now twenty. Where did the time go? Steph and Ben left last year. I was sorry to see them go as we had become a real family of sorts in the home. Still, things move on. Steph started

64

her police training, Ben was ready to settle down in his own permanent home and this was all made possible by the divine intervention of Jenny and Stuart and their Lighthouse charity, who helped with accommodation and childcare. Steph called last week to say that training was going well and that she was due to pass the course and had been offered a secondment in Oxfordshire. Wow! I still can't get my head around that. With everything that she and Ben had been through it was totally amazing to see them doing so well. I am so proud of them both. I miss them a lot.

We currently have Lexi with us and Judy with her two year old twin girls, Amy and Anna. Similar to my own situation, Lexi and Judy came to live with us with very little notice and few belongings – mainly clothes that they were wearing or trinkets that they could carry. However, Lottie and I are very good at getting things together quickly, topping up the food shopping and adjusting sleeping arrangements to ensure a smooth transition to the home for them. We've had a lot of practise over the past few years!

I have had no contact with my mother since the night I decided to leave my home. "Don't look back", that's what Maureen told me on that fateful night. I'm determined not to let everyone down, including myself, but that's a lot of pressure for one person to live up to. I finish off my third sketch of the lamp-post in the summer and start to set up my palate of watercolours, picking out the shades that I want to use to reflect what I want to show. Thankfully, last year Lottie and I decided that I should move to the larger bedroom situated at the front of the house. This room also has an attached bathroom which gives me total privacy. The bedroom gets lots of sun and natural light and helps me to make the most of my sketches and paintings.

My mobile pings. There's a short text. It's Sid from my art class.

Hey, Jem, what you up to? I read.

Just about to start painting project part three. The summer one, I text back.

Do you fancy meeting for a drink later? Well, that's not what I expected.

I look at the words and suddenly Noah's face floods my thoughts. I'm not sure why. It's not like we're in contact anymore, and yet I just can't quite bring myself to say yes to Sid's text.

Can we take a raincheck? Need to get this finished, I reply. That's not really a no, is it? I just need him to hold back for a while so that I can get my head together. These paintings should come first.

Sure, comes the reply. *See you tomorrow.*

Have a good night, I reply, and turn my phone on silent. My thoughts suddenly focus on the canvas that I need to paint.

"Come on, little one," I say to the canvas. "Let's get you finished."

Chapter 12:
Showtime: now (Jem)

Noah and I walk slowly into the living room. I am flanked by Maureen, Stuart and Jenny. My mother, who was sitting on the sofa with Craig, suddenly stands and moves towards me, arms outstretched. A strange move considering I haven't seen her in ten years, apart from our short interlude at the wedding.

"Come here, darling. We've been waiting for you for ages."

I move back a step and Noah steps in front of me, intercepting the fake embrace.

"Joyce," he says, his voice cold. "What are you doing here?"

"Noah?" she says. "Is that you? My, you've grown up good." She looks Noah up and down as if she's wondering whether to eat him or hit him. I don't know whether to throw up or smack her in the face. I do none of those things, just stand there like a lemon.

"Joyce?" he asks again.

"I came to see my daughter of course!" She offers a stilted smile my way.

Craig stands up and uses Noah's distraction with my mother to slither toward me. He gives me a lop-sided grin, a grin he thinks means that I will take pity on him and throw myself into his arms.

"Jem, I don't understand. What happened to you? We were doing okay, weren't we?" He tries to take my arm but I flinch as he touches me. I move out of his reach. Quickly, Maureen moves closer to me.

Noah's voice cuts in. "I wouldn't do that, mate, if I were you."

"Who the hell are you? And what's this got to do with you?"

"What do you mean what happened to me?" I say, my voice rising in anger. "I didn't have a cold or have an accident. I found out that you'd invited my mother to our wedding. On our bloody wedding day of all days. Why would you do that?"

"Joyce wanted to see you. She wanted to get back in touch with you. We thought it would be for the best, to help you get over your hang-ups."

"Hang-ups!" I feel my voice going up several octaves as I shout at him. "Hang-ups! What fucking hang-ups?"

"Jemima, mind your language!" says my mother. "I told you she was volatile. You should have seen her as a kid, nothing but tantrums," she says, looking sweetly at Craig.

"I think we need to talk," Craig says edging closer again. "We can sort this out." He grabs my arm forcibly before I can wrench it away. He's trying to steer me to the front door.

"No!" I say to him calmly but firmly. "I'm going nowhere with you, Craig. Whatever we had or thought we had, it's over. Do you hear me? Over!" What is the matter with this prick? Doesn't he understand English?

Noah steps toward him.

"Last warning. Let. Her. Go."

"Fu–" Craig starts to say but doesn't get very far. Something hard and unrelenting punches him in the face. Noah's fist. If I wasn't so mad at mother and Craig I would have swooned a little over Noah, in the way he's standing here, protecting me. Craig staggers back, clutching his nose with one hand and using the other hand to hold on to the chair to stop himself from falling to the floor.

Joyce rushes to Craig and puts her hands protectively on his shoulders. She is so cross that spittle comes out of her mouth as she lashes out at Noah and me.

"What is the matter with you? He's entitled to speak to his fiance."

"Ex-fiance!" I whip in quickly. "Just like you are my ex-mother. I'm done with the both of you."

Noah stands beside me and somehow we find each other's hands and link fingers. I feel so much stronger than I thought I'd feel. Having him, Maureen, Jenny and Stuart with me has made such a difference. The soft pressure from his fingers remind me that he's here for me.

Stuart sit's in the opposite armchair fiddling with his mobile. He looks unassuming but I know that beneath the harmless exterior he is passionate when protecting those he cares for and those he feels are vulnerable and in danger. He knows I'm vulnerable where my mother is concerned. He looks at Joyce.

"Sit down, Joyce," he says with some authority. "As you're here, I would like to ask you a few questions."

Joyce looks at Noah and then to me. I nod for her to sit and to my surprise she does. Maureen and Jenny have Craig covered as he sits in the chair nursing his bloody nose. I try not to feel sorry for him but it's hard as I stare at the blood splatters on his white shirt.

"How did you meet Craig?"

She looks warily at Craig. "We met at an AA meeting."

I look at Noah and we both shake our heads in disbelief. An AA meeting? Surely they're not both recovering alcoholics? Craig has drunk alcohol since we met, and when we've been out on dates, oh, and then there was that wedding we attended. What an arse!

"When did you meet?" Stuart continues his questioning.

"Two years ago. We had a bit of a fling. It fizzled out and we kept in touch," she says, studying her fingernails as though she doesn't want to make eye contact.

"Hold on a minute," I broke into the conversation. "A fling? You had a fling with HIM?" I point to Craig. "You have got to be fucking kidding me." I cannot believe this. Talk about Jeremy Kyle. Talk about dysfunctional families. How did my life become this farce? I wanted to hit something. Really hard. Then I feel a pressure on my fingers and I'm pulled back into the present and begin to calm myself again.

In my head I'm trying hard to understand what this means as my mind frantically tries to process the time frame. Mother met Craig two years ago and I met him a year ago.

Alarm bells are ringing and getting louder by the minute.

"It was just sex, darling," my mother purrs.

"Why are you bointing at be like that?" Craig fires back, his bloody nose hindering his ability to speak properly. "Why shoulbn't she hab a fling with be? She's a goob-looking woban, I'm a goob-looking ban. We ber both adults and free."

Just thinking of them both together makes me feel queasy. I cannot look at either of them. Instead I look at Jenny and Maureen as they "babysit" Craig.

"Two years ago," I begin. "You met two years ago. Then you met me, Craig. That was convenient. I guess my mother gave you a huge incentive to befriend and develop a relationship with me. The thought of the money must have made it all worthwhile."

"Yes," he says without thinking, "Your mother wanted me to find out about your paintings."

"Shut up, Craig! Not another word, do you hear me?" my mother admonishes him.

"Sorry," he says to her. When I see the way he looks at her it suddenly dawns on me that he still has feelings for her. How can this be? I'm not sure, but there is something lingering there between them. Perhaps he's been caught up in her lies and games. She could easily have used him to help her get information about my painting and net worth. No one wants to believe that their mother could do that to them, but hell – it's what she does, right?

"We know you are the famous artist, Marnie Lake. We know you're worth a bob or two. And we know that you want desperately to keep your alias. I wonder what price you are willing to pay to keep your identity away from the public?" my mother suddenly spits out. Her mouth is running away with her and she can't seem to stop herself.

"Finally." I smile and clap my hands slowly. "At last. The truth."

Jenny and Maureen look at each other, shaking their heads in disbelief.

"You're seriously sitting here attempting to blackmail Jem in front of witnesses." Jenny can't keep the surprise and condemnation out of her voice.

"Wouldn't have had to do this if you'd married me like we'd planned," Craig butted in.

"And you sound really annoyed about that. Fucking prick," Noah says without looking at Craig. Craig eyed him suspiciously. He's about to say something nasty back to Noah but thinks better of it and keeps quiet.

I cannot believe that Craig is blaming me for not falling in with his and my mother's plan. I would have revealed everything to him once we were married. I can't believe how close I had come to trusting this prick.

"Of course, you may choose not to hand any cash over," Mother continues. "Which would be such a shame because we would have to resort to Plan B." She takes an envelope out of her bag and hands it to Stuart. Inside the envelope are photos of the two refuge homes with the addresses handwritten on the back.

Stuart hands the photos to Jenny. She takes one look at the information and photos and her face pales. Slowly she sits down on the sofa.

"So, your Plan B would be to blackmail us to give you money for fear that you will share confidential details of the two domestic violence unit homes that are supported by The Lighthouse charity. What, on social media? Local news?" Stuart's voice turns to steel.

"It's nothing personal. It's just business. I need money and you can provide it," she replies, her eyes never leaving mine.

Noah steps forward and addresses Joyce and Craig.

"You need to leave."

"But we've only just started talking, and, of course, there are copies of those," whines Mother, grinning as though she has won the lottery.

"Get out of my house!" Maureen moves over to Mother and starts to poke her in the chest. "You have always been a mean-spirited, evil woman. I am not sure what happened to you to make you this way. You make me ashamed to know you, Joyce. Now bloody get out of my house. Both of you!"

Mother and Craig both stand. Mother primly puts her bag over her forearm and keeps her chin raised. Craig looks a little shaken, his nose is beginning to swell and it's going to hurt like a month of Sundays tomorrow. Good.

Stuart, Jenny and Maureen start a sort of pincer movement to get the unwanted guests closer to the front door. Once they are over the threshold Maureen closes the door firmly.

"I am going to fucking kill her," Noah says pacing the room. "All she ever does is leave pain and destruction wherever she goes."

Jenny looks at Stuart, holding his phone.

"Did you get it all?" she asks him.

He nods, holding on to the phone. He presses a button and we hear a clear recording of Mother and Craig's visit. Every single threat and every single explanation of her plans to get me married off to Craig so that they could somehow take charge of my money.

"She thinks she knows us," Stuart says, "but she has no idea. No idea at all. She's out of her league." Jenny holds tightly to the envelope. This was going to have to be handled carefully, there were lives at stake if the refuge home addresses were to ever be leaked to the public. Confidentiality and secrecy is the key to living safely and keeping the people inside the homes protected.

We need to find out where Mother and Craig are staying and put together a case of evidence to have them both arrested. Jenny looks at everyone and says quietly, "We'll get Jack on to this immediately. This is our top priority now. We will also need to step up security on the homes until this matter is resolved. Steph will be able to give us some practical advice on where to go from there. Maureen, are you okay if we meet back here tomorrow, at say 2pm?"

Maureen nods.

Noah's phone buzzes. "Shit. It's Suzanne. I'd better get this." He walks off to the hallway, talking quietly into the phone.

I strain to hear what he is saying to her. "Yes, I'll be home soon. I'll pick up pizza on my way. The usual. See you in thirty."

Noah returns as Jenny and Stuart hug us before leaving. He moves toward me and says quietly, "I have to go. I need to talk to Suzanne."

"It's okay. Do what you have to do," I say, trying not to sound too despondent or needy.

"I'll see you tomorrow," he says as his hand caresses my cheek and kisses my forehead.

He gives Maureen a quick hug and then he's gone.

Maureen and I look at each other, each trying not to give a big sigh.

"I'll pop the kettle on," she says. "Things always seem better with a cup of tea."

I slump on the sofa, my head in my hands. I hold onto the words that Noah and I shared with each other earlier today. Are these feelings that we have real? They feel real, but doubts keep running through my mind. I haven't seen Noah in ten years, how can our old feelings have developed into something so deep so quickly? How do we only feel whole when we are together?

Maureen puts the steaming tea mugs on the side table, sits next to me and picks needles and wool from her knitting basket. She talks without looking my way, as though I'm not in the room.

"After you left Noah withdrew into himself. He didn't date, didn't speak much, only when he had to. I was glad when he went to university because I hoped it would make him join in and start living again. You were always good friends, but there was something else, a bond there that even a blind person could see."

I look at my hands, taking in her words.

"That grandson of mine has loved you for ten long years, Jemima. He tried to move forward, he found Suzanne, made a good life for himself. When he bought those paintings, he saw something in them that reminded him of you even though he never knew they were yours. What does that tell you?"

I'm not sure what to say. That it's fate, meant to be?

"I don't know if it was meant to be. I do love him, but what if he's overwhelmed with the idea of me being back here. I don't want him to put me on a pedestal, we need to be real, both of us. We've both lived and sort of loved. In many ways we're different people."

"Of course you are different people. You were nothing but children ten years ago," she says somewhat sternly and then softens. "I'm sure Noah understands that you both have flaws and complicated lives. He needs to speak to Suzanne. It's not fair to keep the girl dangling if his heart isn't in it. Personally, I think his heart belongs to you and always has."

"Yes, I agree." I sip my tea slowly and think over Maureen's words, not quite sure which part of her I agree with. But time will tell.

Chapter 13:
The lamp-post shakers: two years ago (Jem)

There are a million and one things that I need to do to get ready for tonight's tenth anniversary celebration of The Lighthouse charity. I lay the tablecloth and add some serving plates and place cutlery into a large glass. Ten years of offering short-term stay for vulnerable families who need emergency accommodation and support from people they can trust. Ten years to have appreciated and benefited from a lifelong friendship with Jenny, Stuart, Lottie and Claire who runs the second domestic violence refuge home. They are the family that some of us have never had. I know that I'm grateful for my second family. I am the exception in some ways. I came to Shore House and I stayed.

Jenny, Stuart and Lottie have this theory. It's silly really, one of our little Saturday night chats when we right the world's wrongs over a glass of wine. They know about my lamp-post projects and know the fascination I have in the way they are depicted in the light. Anyway, back to the Saturday night theory. They believe that the lamp-post is symbolic of a person standing proud, standing strong, the bright light that lives within us relating to the essence of our uniqueness and strength. No matter what tries to shake us, change us or move us, we stand with our heads held high and strive to be the best that we can be in life.

To those lamp-post shakers who make every effort to undermine, hurt and violate, you will not win. Because we are strong. We are not alone. We have friends, we develop new families, and as a unit we are invincible. My mother, the lamp-post shaker, Old Pete the sleazeball. Don't mind me, I'm just musing. To be honest, I like the theory too.

My mobile buzzes. It's Chloe, my agent. I pick up the phone and her excited voice screeches through the speaker, hurting my ear a little.

"Jem! Jem! You won't believe this…but someone just walked into the gallery. It's crazy…."

"Calm down, Chloe. Tell me slowly," I say patiently.

"You know Joel Richmond from the rock band Drako Spark?"

"Yes…"

"Well," she continues, "he lives near the gallery and he popped in to browse for some artwork for his new house in the Cotswolds. He's just bought your 'Seasons' set – the lamp-post pictures."

"No way! You're kidding me!" I find the dining table chair and gingerly sit down.

"Yes way. I'm telling you. I told you years ago that your work was brilliant. That's why I've got so many of your pieces here. That's also why I pay you to work for two days a week at the gallery so that you can carry on sketching, painting and drawing for the rest of the week – to carry on developing your art and inspiration."

Lottie comes into the kitchen carrying a handful of blown up balloons and some serviettes. She looks at me. I raise my eyebrows to her and shake my head.

"Okay. So, let me get this straight. Joel Richmond just bought a set of four of my paintings?"

"Yes. I was about to barter with him over the cost, when he slapped a cheque on my desk and said, *'I want the Lamp-post collection. Can you get them to me today? This should cover it. Whoever this Marnie Lake is she had better hold tight, because I'm not finished buying her stuff and I think she's going to go viral. My mates are going to dig this work.'* He asked for my card and said that he is coming back next week with some of his friends to take another look around."

"How much was on the cheque?" I ask quietly.

"£50,000."

"£50,000!" I repeat! "Holy Cow!" I couldn't believe what I was hearing.

"Holy Cow indeed!" Chloe replied, and suddenly we were both jumping up and down and laughing down the phone. Lottie rushes to me and hugs me tightly.

"Oh my god, oh my god! I'm so proud of you," she keeps saying.

"Chloe? You still there?" I say into my mobile. "Thank you so much! For believing in me and my work. I'll see you tomorrow."

I hear Chloe choke up a little as though she's feeling overwhelmed.

"This is a once in a lifetime thing, Jem. Thank you for letting me join you on this journey. See you tomorrow."

"Sure will."

Marnie Lake has entered the building and I can't stop smiling.

"We need to remember to keep your identity a secret tonight at the party. There are going to be quite a few people who have volunteered, been supported and lived in the two homes here tonight. Perhaps we can say that Chloe rang and was so pleased that she's sold her paintings to a rock star. No one needs to know that you are Marnie Lake," Lottie warns as she takes the sausage rolls out of the oven. They smell heavenly.

"Jenny, Stuart and Claire are going to be so pleased for you. I'm so pleased for you I could burst!" Lottie smiles as she transfers the sausage rolls onto a wire rack to cool down.

Sasha walks in with her six month old baby girl, Zoe, on her shoulder as she gently burps her. She's sixteen and had been living with her parents. She had hoped that they could accept her pregnancy and support and cherish their new granddaughter, but it was not to be. Her dad decided that he couldn't cope with the stigma, noise, bother – whatever – so he punched Sasha in the face in a fit of rage and told her and the baby to get out. Apparently, this wasn't the first time. They'd arrived two days ago. Her facial bruises are beginning to come out more as is the swelling. It must have been quite a big punch and the damage to her emotional well-being may never be repaired.

"Sit down, Sasha, I'm just about to pop the kettle on," I say, pulling out a chair for her and motioning for her to sit.

"Everything okay with Zoe?" Lottie asks. Sasha's eyes are red as if she's been crying. Lottie and I notice this but say nothing. The first few days are the hardest, often you're hurting physically as well as mentally, you're weary, despondent and you're usually responsible for a child or baby. The transition support time into the home is vital. It's important for Sasha to know that she and the baby are safe and that their basic needs are cared for.

"Do you need a hand?" Lottie asks quietly.

Sasha bursts into tears, wipes her nose and eyes on her jumper and allows Lottie to take Zoe. Zoe coos in Lottie's arms as she rocks her gently.

"You know you're doing a great job with her, right?" I say to Sasha. "But never be afraid to ask for help. That's what we're here for. You're not in this alone now." I go to her, bend down and give her the warmest hug I can. "Our hugs are not rationed you know. You get to have one anytime you need one."

Lottie smiles at me. I nod back at her.

"Now, let's make that cup of tea," I say, rising and heading to the kettle.

Many hours later I'm in my room reflecting on Chloe's news and on the celebratory evening. Jenny, Stuart, Lottie and

Claire were genuinely pleased for me and raised a glass of champagne quietly when there was a lull in the kitchen to salute my very first sale. Silently I am still in a state of disbelief that anyone, especially a rock star, would be interested in my work.

I have decided that I am going to give some of my earnings to The Lighthouse charity. Obviously, this depends on what I receive from Chloe after she has taken her commission. That's my plan.

The party guests were former residents, staff and volunteers. It was great to catch up with women and children who had lived at Shore House, seeing what had become of them and what they had achieved. The human spirit never ceases to amaze me when it comes to its ability to overcome adversity. It makes you feel emotional and proud of being part of the process of caring for those who are in need.

One of the best surprises of the evening was to see Steph and Ben walk in through the door as we were unsure if they were able to attend. Lottie and I had rushed forward at the same time and held them tightly, tears of happiness rolling down our faces.

I stare out of my bedroom window and feel a surge of happiness and contentment as my eyes move slowly toward the lamp-post, its strong metal base rising to the top to the light bulb and cover where it shines bright, strong and proud. I'm here and I'm still standing.

Chapter 14:
The boy done good: two years ago (Noah)

This is it. It's really happening. I can't believe I'm finally here. I look around the room, it's empty but for a small mahogany desk sitting in the corner. I'm holding the keys to my new office and apartment. I jingle the keys between my fingers so they make a clinking sound, and I can't help but smile with satisfaction as I acknowledge the physical sign that I've finally got my own place. This is my new chapter. I hear shuffling, huffing and puffing and then Charlie bursts into the room with two boxes stacked on top of each other. At least I think it's Charlie, I can't quite see his face!

"Let me take one of those from you." I grab a box and put it carefully on the desk.

"Jesus, Noah, how much stuff have you got?" he says, putting his box next to mine on the desk. It's good of Charlie to give me a hand. He's a good mate. He studied English and creative writing at university and is now one of the publishers at a large firm nearby.

"I know there's a lot but I've got a lot of stuff because I'm trying to sort the office and the living area upstairs. The filing cabinet and chairs, small sofa, printer and a table are arriving tomorrow. The phone line should already be connected, I'll check when I find the new phone I've bought but it's been boxed. It's got to be somewhere close," I rambled as my head spins at a hundred miles per hour.

I got a first for my law degree and still remember that bittersweet moment as I walked on the stage in my graduation gown to see Gran and Charlie smiling and waving madly at me, instead of my parents. Life can be a bitch sometimes.

If Jem were here what would she say? She'd tell me to stop wallowing and pull myself together. Well, that's what I'm doing. Where did that come from? I haven't thought of her in years. I tell myself that she's part of my past and that's where she needs to stay.

"Shall we finish getting the rest of the boxes in and then pop to the pub for a pint and some lunch?" Charlie always knows when to say the right thing.

My mobile buzzes and I smile at Gran's text message. *Hope things go well today. I'm so proud of you. Your mum and dad would have been too. See you Thursday, Gran xx.* I quickly respond with a *Thanks* and *See you Thursday x* and pop the mobile in my back pocket.

"Sure, why not?" I say, determined to get on top of this moment so I can finally enjoy what I've worked so hard for.

We head back to the van that Charlie's borrowed for the day and collect the rest of the stuff. I didn't know I had so many clothes! I must remember to check to see if I have enough smart shirts and trousers. I don't want to start the business off on the wrong foot. I remember the apartment and office keys in my pocket and make a mental note to get a spare set of each. It would be good to get some sort of signage for the company, though I'm still struggling to think of a name. Perhaps I should just call it "N. Robinson – Solicitors".

In the end I decided to use the money from the sale of my parents' house, my childhood home, to buy this centre of town ready-made office with an upstairs, self-contained loft-style apartment.

I couldn't settle to living at my old home without my parents after uni. Too many memories. The feeling of sadness and emptiness within my childhood home made me feel despondent and claustrophobic. I guess it just didn't feel like home anymore, so I moved in with Gran. It killed two birds with one stone, I wouldn't be so lonely, and I could keep an eye on Gran and help her more as she got older. We stored sentimental furniture and objects safely and carefully at her house. It was enough to have my personal possessions around me. The rest of the stuff I sold.

Finally, we finish lugging the boxes into the house and walk to the pub on the corner.

"I'm getting these. You've done enough today. Couldn't have done this without your help, mate," I say patting Charlie on the back.

Once the food is ordered we find a quiet corner to sit back and re-charge our batteries.

"Do you ever think of her?" Charlie suddenly says.

"Who?" I ask

"Jem," he replies.

"Sometimes," I nod, looking at him. "Do you?"

"Yes. Sometimes. I wonder where she is and what happened to make her leave like that."

"I don't know, mate," I admit.

"I saw the bruises and scars you know."

"They were hard to ignore, weren't they? It's not like she tried to hide them. I should have done something to help her, maybe she would've stayed." Not sure if I'm talking to Charlie or myself.

"I hope she's happy wherever she is," he says suddenly.

Charlie picks up his pint and says, "Here's to Jem. We hope you're out there somewhere and that you're okay." I clink my glass with his. *Ditto, mate, ditto...*

Charlie picks up his pint again. "Cheers to you, mate. You done good."

"We both did, mate. We both did," I say, clinking again. Charlie, my mate the publisher, from childhood friends to grown-ups, yeah – we did good. We're both independent and have good career pathways. It can only get better from here.

"You know," I mused, "once I get everything in place, I'm going to need to brighten the office and apartment up with some good pieces of artwork."

"A friend I know recommends a nice little art gallery in Dorchester that she uses. Perhaps we could go visit one day. Make a day of it when we can tie in our work schedules."

"Forget about organising it. Let's just do it," I say. "*Carpe diem.*"

"Road trip," Charlie smiles. "Let finish up here and head off then."

Two hours later we pull up into a quaint tree-lined side road just off the centre of Dorchester. The sign on the window says "Impressions Artists". The window is dressed using a variety of carefully displayed artwork and looks good. We open the door and the bell swings to let the manager know that someone has entered the shop.

I love looking at art. I love the different styles and the colours. I always told myself that when I had my own place that I would treat myself to a few pieces of art.

I wander around taking in the beautiful pieces of work. Some of them are so big that they will fill my entire office wall! I'm not sure what I'm looking for but I'm hopeful that something will wow me enough to buy it for my new place.

Suddenly, I reach a collection of watercolours and sketches and my heart starts to beat fast. My hands feel clammy, I don't know why, I've never had a reaction like this before from looking at paintings. Well, apart from when I found Jem's sketches in her notebook. I am mesmerised by the strokes as the pencil and charcoal flow across the canvas. The collection ranges from sketches and watercolours of the surf as it comes onto the beach, and sketches of the lighthouse at Portland Bill to the famous harbour around Lyme Regis. I think it's called "The Cobb". You know the one in the Jane Austen novels? I look closer to see the name of the artist – Marnie Lake. Nice name. The caption on the canvas says simply *Famous*.

"This collection is from a local artist, Marnie Lake," a woman's voice breaks into my thoughts. "I'm Chloe Green, this is my gallery."

I stand still looking at the name. I'm not sure why, but I suddenly feel a chill go through me.

"Marnie Lake, she's very collectable at the moment. People seem to really love her work. She's one to look out for. I sold a set of four paintings last week to a famous rock star," she says with pride.

"I'll take it," I say, pointing to the painting of the harbour.

"Seen something you like, mate?" Charlie says, walking toward us.

"Yep. This one. I'm buying it," I say, feeling excited and point to the painting with the harbour at Lyme Regis in it.

Chloe, the owner, carefully takes the painting from the wall, walks to the counter and begins to slowly wrap it in parcel wrap and string. Jesus, I haven't even checked the price. It won't make a difference I tell myself, I've got to have it.

I hand my credit card over to Chloe and we go through the familiar chip and pin routine with the card machine.

She hands me the wrapped painting and we make our way back to the car.

"Jesus, mate. Can't believe you just spent £2,000.00 on a painting!"

"Me neither," I laugh, holding the painting close to me.

I love this painting. It's going in my dining room area. I can't explain it, but it feels like it's meant to be with me, it's meant to be there. I may need to start building up my law business fast, I've got a feeling that this isn't going to be the only painting I purchase from Marnie Lake!

Chapter 15:
Three shots too many: two years ago (Joyce)

Silence. It's so quiet. I sit looking at this dump of a place. It's an old seventies style community centre and we're sitting on metal pull-out chairs that clatter across the floor every time someone moves. There are seven of us tonight, sitting in a circle. Thankfully, my head is numbed by the three straight vodka shots that I drank before coming here.

I've been trying to get off the booze for a while now, and despite the vodka shots I think I'm doing well. Still, it's hard. There's an empty chair next to me and a woman on the other side. She shuffles, scraping her chair, and I cringe. God that noise goes through me. I take a deep breath and count to ten. I ask myself again why I'm here. My original idea was to sort my drinking problem out so that Pete will take me back. But if I'm honest he's a bit of a sleazeball. I mean, the way he looked at Jemima the night before she left, it made me cringe. He's not worth the effort. My original plan has changed.

There was a time when life wasn't too bad. When I had a husband and a daughter. But he turned out to be a loser, went to work one day and never came back. Disappeared off the face of the earth. I blamed Jemima of course. Ted's leaving was all her fault. If we hadn't been saddled with a child we would have had a chance at life, at living. That girl had the devil in her, I could see it. She was always challenging me, always giving me grief. Still, it was nice to have her around sometimes, especially when I'd come home from work and she'd have dinner ready.

The problem was I couldn't control myself around her. There was an anger in me, a fierce need to hurt her and put her in her place. I don't know where the need came from. It was just there.

Back to my new plan. I need to find a new man. Someone with prospects, with money. Someone who will look after me. Maybe these meetings will help me find someone. You never know. I can always "bump him off" if he gets on my nerves.

Kris, the group leader, sits in his usual chair and crosses his legs.

"Welcome, everyone. Good to see you." A few people are still checking their mobiles but nod at him anyway.

"Tonight we have a new member. Everyone, please welcome Craig to the group."

A tall, red-headed man stares awkwardly at his feet. He's not my type but beggars can't be choosers.

"Please find a seat. Anywhere will do," Kris says to Craig.

Craig notices the empty chair to the one side of me and slowly heads my way. Promising. Very promising. I smile at him. He smiles back.

"Shall we start? Joyce, would you like to go first?" asks Kris.

I stand up. "Hi, my name's Joyce and I'm an alcoholic."

Craig stares at me. He looks like he's way out of his comfort zone. Admitting you have a problem isn't easy. It will take him some time. Maybe I can help him and have a little fun at the same time. You never know. I sidle up to him during the break, helping myself to a coffee.

"How are you doing?" I ask. "It's all a bit much at the beginning, isn't it?"

He nods, admitting honestly, "I guess it makes you face the reality of what you've become. It's not a nice feeling." He's not a happy bunny, you can see that in his face. This man needs a woman.

"It's hard to maintain a normal life when everything becomes about the next drink. Even work suffers," I say, showing understanding and support. Let's hook him in slowly.

"Yeah, I'm an accountant at a small firm and it's getting harder to hide my drinking behaviour. I need to get on top of this so that I don't lose my job and my house."

He's an accountant. He's got his own house. That's got to be good, right?

"Do you fancy grabbing a coffee sometime?" I ask. Might as well get in there quickly. Can't afford to miss any opportunities at my age. Craig gives me an innocent smile as he stirs milk in his polystyrene tea cup.

"That would be good," his deep voice replies.

Game, set and match.

Chapter 16:
Be true to yourself: now (Noah)

Not sure how my life has become so unrecognisable in just twenty-four hours. A complete 360 degree turn about, that's what it is! How had I gone from being in a stable five-month relationship with someone as pretty, clever and sweet as Suzanne to an instant full-on heartstopping love affair with someone who I used to have a close friendship with ten years ago? It doesn't make sense.

I look at the clock. It's 5.30pm. The pizza sits on the dining table in my apartment. I look at my mobile. Suzanne texted to say that she was stuck in traffic and will be a little late. My eyes are drawn to the *Famous* Cobb painting on my dining room wall. The Marnie Lake wave painting *Free*, which was anything but free, stands proudly over the mantlepiece. Jesus, it's been here all along. The answer has been here all along. I've been collecting these paintings because they remind me of Jem. Jem who is Marnie Lake. I had a little piece of her with me all this time and never knew it. Christ, how spooky is that.

Okay, it's time to be honest with myself. I see Jem, her face, her body, her clothes. I see her worried, happy, cross, angry. But in the end, if I'm honest, what I really see is the other half of me. The bit that sees her is the replica of what she sees in me. Our souls are connected, intertwined, I don't know how, I don't know why. It scares me.

I don't want to hurt Suzanne, I'm not that kind of guy. I'm desperately trying to find the right words in my head so that I can tell Suzanne. It's as clear as day. My heart beats for Jem. I love her.

The key being turned in the lock as the apartment door opens breaks into my thoughts. *Be true to yourself, Noah* I tell myself. This is going to be hard. I take a deep breath.

"Hey, Suze," I say, rising from my comfy chair. I move toward her and skim a kiss on her cheek.

"I got pepperoni."

"Thanks, babe." She smiles and strokes my cheek. God, hurting this woman is going to break me. I'm not sure if I can do it.

"Before we eat I need to tell you something. Can you sit, it's important." I begin, beckoning her to sit on the sofa next to me. There's no backing out now. No matter what happens, I'm going with my gut and ultimately that leads me to Jem. *I'm so sorry, Suzanne. I never meant to hurt you.*

Suzanne puts her handbag on the sofa and sits down with a worried look on her face.

"You okay, babe?"

"I'm fine," I reassure her.

And I begin an abbreviated story of my life with Jem. How she left home when she was fifteen and how our lives had never really fully recovered from the separation. I told her that Jem had come back into my life and that this was something that I needed to explore. I didn't reveal the real name of the artist of the paintings that adorn my walls and bring me so much joy. I didn't embellish too much because I didn't feel it necessary to be too graphic with my feelings. I didn't want to hurt Suzanne any more than I had to.

I look up. My head had been resting in my hands and she's moved to the opposite end of the sofa. I feel like such a shit for doing this to her. Suzanne is crying.

"I'm so sorry, Suze, really I am," I say, my heart sinking. Still she says nothing.

Finally, she looks at me and says the words I knew she would say.

"Noah, you are a complete and utter bastard!" We both stand up, staring warily at each other. Then she takes one step so that she is face to face with me, swings her right hand and slaps me hard across the face.

She grabs her bag and rushes to the front door. She looks back at me to make her final parting speech "This is a big mistake. What you feel for this girl can't possibly be real. But you've had your chance. Do not come running back to me when this all falls apart!"

I hear the door slam and slump back into a chair. I didn't want her to go this way, but this was my choice, my decision, and I needed to let her lead the way as it finished. I deserved everything she said and did. I was a bastard. I hadn't even given a thought to what having her as a business partner would mean if we ever split up. Stupid, stupid man.

I grab the bottle of Jack Daniels from the kitchen cupboard, unscrew the lid and tip it slowly into my mouth. The bottle comes with me to the sofa as I find the TV remote, switch on Netflix and carry on sipping.

My mobile buzzes. There's a text from Charlie.

What the fuck, Noah? What did you do to Suzanne? She's just texted, sounds like she's in tears.

I ignore the text and the next one. My head starts to go a little fuzzy as the sweet liquor does its job of slowing my thoughts and making my head heavy.

I look at the painting over the mantlepiece as some superhero with an iron fist fights the bad guys. *Free.* It's like she knows what I'm doing, what I'm going through. In my stupor I know I'm being true to myself, I know that this is just the beginning, and I know that things will work out okay in the end. Still, what I wouldn't give for Jem to be here right now, her arms around me and telling me that everything will be alright.

Another buzz from my mobile. Something makes me check it. It's a text from Jem.

You okay? It's Jem.

No, but I will be, I reply

I'm so sorry.

Don't' be.

Perhaps it would be better for everyone if I leave.

Is that what you want to do? I dread her reply.

No. I want to stay. I want you.

This lifts me. Gives me hope.

I love you, Jem. I text the words I've been afraid to say to her. I need her to know. Can't waste any more time taking things slowly.

The moments pass and I think I've frightened her away. Then my mobile starts to ring. I'm hoping it's Jem. Her name flashes on the screen and I swipe to answer the call. My ear is against the earpiece and I listen with bated breath as her soft voice soothes my heavy heart, saying the words that I've been hoping to hear.

"I love you too, Noah. I always have and always will." I can't stop smiling as I listen to her words.

"It's good to hear your voice. I ended it with Suzanne tonight," I say.

"I guessed as much. Try to get some rest. I know you feel bad about Suzanne, I feel bad about it too. One day at a time, that's what you said."

"One day at a time. I love you," I repeat.

"I know. Goodnight. See you tomorrow." Her voice is quiet and calm.

"Tomorrow," I whisper, and we both hang up.

Feeling much better I slow down on the Jack Daniels and make my way to the almost cold pizza. Bringing the box to the sofa, I take out a slice of pepperoni and settle down for a few hours. I'll call Charlie tomorrow and let him know what's happened.

Chapter 17:
An expected surprise: one year ago
(Jem)

I love this coffee shop. The delicious aroma from my latte, the friendliness of the staff and the ability to sneak into a corner to enjoy my Kindle, helps me to keep my mojo so that I can spend most of my time painting and sketching. I work in Chloe's art gallery on Wednesdays and Fridays. Sometimes if I'm in the middle of a project I'll take a few days off. Chloe is an angel, she knows that I need to have this flexibility so that I can continue to paint and sketch.

I still cannot believe that Marnie Lake's paintings are selling pretty much like hot cakes. Following Joel's purchase of the Lamp-post collection, he seems to be almost single-handedly sending clients my way. Chloe is so pleased. I don't think she ever expected this amount of notoriety or success from the Marnie Lake artwork.

She's spending a lot of time with Joel and we've agreed that she will never reveal my true identity to him. I trust her. If my mother were to ever find out that there was money to be made from her idle, good-for-nothing, difficult daughter she would be here in a flash trying to latch on to anything she can get.

My Kindle is great for escapism. I can forget my world for a while and become embroiled in a romance, adventure or thriller to allow my mind to slow and delve into something that doesn't have timelines or pressures from the outside world. I'm currently reading *Outlander*, which is a big, I mean, massive hulk of a book! It's pretty good. Strange thing though, for some reason – in my mind's eye, Jamie looks just like Noah!

My mobile buzzes and I see that it's Jenny checking in with me via text. Her usual media. I reply explaining that everything is fine. Ever since Joel bought my first paintings I have donated annually to The Lighthouse to help maintain funds. I'm also a silent partner and attend regular meetings to see what needs to be done and developing action plans to achieve set targets.

With my healthy bank balance in mind, I'm looking to move out of Shore House soon and invest in a place of my own. That will be weird, right? Shore House has always had people coming and going but I feel that it's the right time for me to invest in something that's just mine. Lottie and Jenny are visiting a couple of properties with me tomorrow. I'm really looking forward to viewing the Victorian Frampton house. It looks great in the photos. Who knows, this time next year I could own my own home!

I sip the last dregs of my latte and carry on reading about Jamie and Claire. Suddenly a presence looms over my shoulder. It's a man. He's wearing a red T-shirt and black jeans and sports a mop of short red hair. Not bad looking if you like that sort of thing.

"Sorry to bother you." He has a deep voice. "But do you think I could charge my lap top in that socket just by your legs?" He points to the socket under the table on the wall. I didn't even know the socket existed!

"Yes, no problem." I shuffle my chair to one side so that he has access to the plug.

"Do you mind if I sit for a few minutes? Just need to finish this email. It's important."

I look at him. For goodness sake, can't he see that I'm engrossed in my Kindle. I'm careful to keep my face from showing my real feelings. I count to ten and nod.

"Knock yourself out."

The man seems intent on sitting at my table. Not sure why, I haven't given him any signals to say that I'm interested. I'm not one for chit-chat, never have been. I carry on reading my Kindle while listening to the faint sound of keys being tapped.

"There, that's done." He gets up, heads to the bar, says something to a member of staff and points to me. A few minutes later he's back with two steaming mugs.

"Large latte," he says, carefully putting a large mug in front of me. "I asked the bar staff if they could remember what you were drinking. It's the least I could do for interrupting your reading."

As his words register a slither of warmth toward him comes over me. That was sweet of him. He didn't have to do that.

"Thanks. There was no need." I smile.

"I'm Craig by the way."

"Ma...erm...Jem." Damn, where did that come from? I've never used my alias before.

"Nice to meet you, Ma...erm...Jem." He smirks and raises his mug.

"You too, Craig. It's Jem, just Jem." I raise my mug slightly then take a sip. It's delicious.

This almost seems like normal. I've never had normal. Most of my life is made of up various intrigues and untruths, almost all of them to keep me safe and protect whatever assets I have accumulated over the years.

"What do you think are the odds of me asking you out and you saying yes?" he asks.

"Oh, about fifty-fifty," I reply.

"Not good enough, think I've crashed and burned," he smiles, quoting the famous *Top Gun* line.

"Not totally, Maverick. Stick at it and you may increase the odds." Can't believe I'm flirting with this guy. This guy who I've only just met.

"Yes, ma'am!" He salutes offering a big smile.

"I've got tickets for a band playing at a local bar tomorrow. They're good. Want to go with me?" Wow! He's asking me on a date! This is beyond weird.

My common sense tells me to be careful, but this little devil on my shoulder shouts *Go, girl, be spontaneous. Enjoy yourself for once. Live a little.* Before I have time to change my mind, my mouth opens and the words, "Sounds good. I'd be happy to go with you," come out.

We exchange mobile numbers and agree to meet at the bar at 7pm the following night. I am so proud of myself for being spontaneous with this man that I can't stop smiling.

Go, girl, you surprise even yourself sometimes.

Chapter 18:
The world comes to a standstill: now (Jem)

Hello? Hello? Is that Jeremy Kyle? I need your help. I've got a situation. Where do I start? First, there's my estranged mother who hates me and is blackmailing me for money. Oh, she also knows about the two domestic violent refuge homes that I'm connected to and is threatening my friends to give her money so that she doesn't reveal their addresses on social and print media. Secondly, it turns out that the man who I was going to marry also knows her and that they were in a sexual relationship.

Finally, my old childhood friend has turned out to be my soulmate and the love of my life. He's in a relationship with another woman, or was, and now we've got to sort out our feelings for each other as well as sorting out my mother and ex-fiance. Can you help?

A sound jolts me back to reality. A stone hits my bedroom window. I get up off the bed and walk to the window just as another stone hits the window. I see a mop of red hair as Craig stoops behind a small bush that clearly is not tall enough to hide him from the neck up. Dipstick.

"Jem!" he whisper calls. "Jem!"

I open the window and lean out. I'm too tired to deal with Craig today.

"What do you want, Craig?" I shout, annoyance seeping into my words.

"I want to talk to you. Come to the door."

"No."

"Please."

I nod, giving in. I move away from the window and head downstairs to the front door. Maureen watches me with interest as I open the door and stand guard in the doorway. *It's Craig,* I mouth to her. She tuts, walks into the kitchen and starts to fill the washing machine with laundry.

"Okay, you can come out from behind the bush, Craig," I mutter as he skulks into view, his nose looking a little worse for wear after yesterday and reminding me of Noah's protective punch. Be still my beating heart. I know you shouldn't condone acts of violence, but Craig so deserved what he got.

"Say what you have to say, I have things to do," I say without emotion. How did I ever think that I could love this man?

"I think you're being unfair," he begins. "You've given up on us."

"Given up on us!" I repeat. "You screwed up big time and you call me unfair? Stop being such a prick, Craig. The deed is done. On top of that, you screwed my mother! And you're both trying to blackmail me and my friends. We. Are. Over. There. Is. No. Us. Now please leave."

"The blackmail has nothing to do with me, Jem. This is all your mother."

"You are a fool for letting her use you, Craig."

"Maybe, but at least I didn't go running back to my old boyfriend!" His voice has risen an octave.

"I did not!" I shout back at him and then, as if this moment couldn't get any worse, Noah arrives. Great! Before I can say anything Noah nods at Craig, leans in to me and kisses me on the cheek. I lean into the kiss. *Can we freeze this moment?*

"Hey, you," he says in a low husky voice.

"Hey you," I whisper back.

"Excuse me! What the hell?" blusters Craig. Oh dear, I'd forgotten about him.

"Sorry, Craig, but you need to leave," I say.

"Looks like I had a lucky escape," he sneers. "I'm glad I found out what a slut you were before we actually married!"

"Say that again," Noah growls, fists forming ready to pounce. I immediately hold his arms so that he doesn't hit him again. Craig puts his hands to his face to protect himself and storms off.

"Prick!" I shout after him and steer Noah into the house.

"And good riddance!" Maureen's voice shouts from the kitchen.

Noah kisses Maureen on the cheek and gives her a quick hug. We put together some sandwiches and stuff for lunch and help Maureen with chores. It's almost like I never left. The phone rings and I go to answer it but Maureen gets there first.

"Joyce," she says, "I thought it might be you." She looks at me then at Noah. "You want £10,000 transferred into your account by midnight tonight. You want me to write down your account details. Have you gone out of your bloody mind?"

I gently take the phone from Maureen.

"Mother, why are you upsetting Maureen?" I ask, trying as hard as I can not to shout at her. I breathe slowly and continue. "This thing, whatever it is, is between you and me. No one else. You should have kept Craig out of this."

"But, darling, this thing, whatever it is, only works if it involves everyone and everything that's important to you. How else will I get money?"

"I think we need to meet, Mother, just you and me. We need to sort this out once and for all."

"More meetings, darling, will that help? Give you time to get the money? I suppose I can find some time in my busy diary to meet with you."

"I'll meet you at 4pm at the lighthouse at Portland Bill."

"No, darling, that will not do at all," she replies.

"It's 4pm at the lighthouse or you get nothing at all," I say and put the phone down.

106

I stand still, fuming, and wondering what on earth I'm going to do with the woman who calls herself my mother. I feel cold and numb. In a second Noah is here, arms wrapped around me and holding me tight. His strength bolsters me and I slide my arms around his neck. Whatever my next move is with my mother, I need to believe that my relationship with Noah is solid. It's one less thing to worry about.

How will I get £10,000 by midnight tonight? My mind whirls as I start thinking about various ways to swap money into different accounts to give my mother what she wants. The doorbell rings and Maureen rushes to the door to answer it.

Noah tips my chin up and looks into my eyes. "You're not meeting her on your own." I shake my head because I know need to meet her on my own.

"Let's see what Jenny and Stuart think when they get here."

"What we think of what?" Jenny says as she walks into the lounge carrying cakes and biscuits. Noah and I pull away from each other.

Stuart follows her in, and then someone who I haven't seen for a while steps out from behind him.

"Steph!" I shout, running to her, throwing my arms around her and holding her for the longest time.

"Jem!" Steph returns the hug. I'm not sure why she's here but I'm so glad to see her.

"Good to see you," I smile. As astute as ever, she looks around the room to Maureen and Noah.

"This is Maureen. She's was always there for me when I was younger. She contacted Jenny, gave me a second chance. She's the mother I never had." I put my arm around Maureen and feel the emotions well within her. She sniffles and kisses me on the cheek.

Steph moves to Maureen, places her hand on top of Maureen's arm and says simply, "You. Are. A. Good. Woman."

"And this is–"

"Noah," she says with some confidence. "I cannot tell you," she looks at Noah, "how many times I have wondered about you. You had this girl's back and for that alone I respect you." I tear up a little listening to Steph complimenting my adopted family.

Noah shuffles his feet, a little embarrassed, but I can see a gleam in his eyes, a brightness that comes with his shy smile. He doesn't know this woman, but already he's adapting to yet another new situation.

We all move to the kitchen and I go to fill the kettle. As I turn the kettle on Jenny starts putting the mugs, tea, coffee etc on a tray. My mobile buzzes. It's Chloe asking me if everything is okay. I quickly text back to say that I'll call her later. Once we're seated around the table pouring drinks Steph starts talking.

"So, here's where we are at the moment. I've got Stu's recording of the blackmail from last night. This is hard evidence and speaks for itself. Sorry to say this, Jem, but I think Craig was the patsy who Joyce pushed to involve himself with you for your money. We all know how manipulative people can be, her focus is totally on the money. It was a given that you would eventually reveal to Craig that you are Marnie Lake."

"Jack says she's staying with Craig at the Premier Inn just outside Weymouth. He's also found out that Joyce is on the verge of losing the house due to her non-payment of mortgage because of her alcoholism. Don't ask, Steph, best you don't know," Stuart adds.

"Don't tell me. I don't want to know. Jack sounds like my kind of guy though!"

That explains what she wants the money for. It appears that going to AA meetings hasn't worked very well for Joyce. I look at my watch, still very much aware that I'm supposed to be meeting her within an hour and that she wants £10,000 by midnight tonight. There's no way I'm going to let her reveal valuable information about The Lighthouse charity. I wonder if we can get Jack to check her hotel room while I'm meeting her.

"Which reminds me, we were talking earlier about my mother's phone call. I'm going to meet her at the lighthouse in Portland Bill at 4pm. I need to go soon. She wants £10,000 by midnight tonight."

"How do we know that she won't try to blackmail you or us on a regular basis?" asks Noah. "It's not going to work. I also don't think that you should meet your mother alone. Stuart, Jenny, can you get Jack to check Joyce's hotel room for The Lighthouse details and any blackmail evidence? I don't trust her or Craig one inch."

"Good idea," Stuart agrees as he looks at Jenny. They work as one as she dials Jack's number and fires quick instructions to him over the phone.

Steph looks at me. "You cannot meet her alone, Jem. Promise me." Maureen puts her arm around my shoulder and presses tight. I know she's worried about me and a pang of guilt shoots through me as, not for the first time since arriving on her doorstep, I wish I'd somehow managed to keep her away from my chaotic life. She seems to have spent a lifetime worrying about me in one way or another, this woman who knew that I needed someone to care about me. Noah turns to catch my eye, his hand on my thigh and mouths, *I'm coming with you.*

I stare back into his blue eyes and know without a doubt this is something that I need to do by myself. If I don't stand up to her now I am giving her carte blanche to make mischief in the future. Sometimes you have to stand up and be counted, right? I am not a child anymore, she cannot hurt me physically or mentally. This was my time.

Steph rises from her chair and looks at the clock.

"My sergeant is aware of the situation and will give us further advice as needed. Under no circumstances should any of you give her or Craig any money. Not a penny. I have started the paperwork to build a case of blackmail against them and have handed it to a friend in CID. Blackmail is a statutory offence in this country. Jem, I need to get to work, I'm on the afternoon shift. Noah, can I have a quick word?"

Noah removes his hand from my thigh and I'm surprised by how unsettled I feel without his touch. I miss it, it calms me. I stand quickly and hug Steph, muttering a thank you for her help, then she and Noah walk to the front door. I stand up, I'd better get myself ready to go and meet the mother from hell.

Stuart, Jenny and Maureen walk to the front door to say goodbye and thank Steph.

Noah returns and walks me upstairs where I need to pick up a cardigan. "Let me come with you, Jem? Please," he says quietly. I know he wants to protect me but I'll be fine. It's daylight, it's a public place. What danger can I be in?

"Sorry, Noah, but I have to do this. You need to let me do this. Perhaps I can reason with her."

He laughs bitterly and shakes his head.

"Like that has ever happened. Promise me you won't put yourself in any unnecessary danger." He presses his forehead to mine. We rest against each other for a quiet moment until I pull away. I have to go, this is on me and I need to at least try to sort it out.

"I promise."

I head downstairs and to the door.

"I'll be back in a few hours," I tell everyone and shut the door behind me.

What I don't see is Maureen stepping forward with a set of car keys.

"Remember the old Fiesta, the one you're still insured on?" she says to Noah. He nods and takes the car keys.

Chapter 19:
It's a funny business: now (Joyce)

"Yes!" I say, rubbing my hands together. I can almost smell the money. I sip my fifth glass of vodka as I congratulate myself on finally getting one over on my good-for-nothing daughter. The problem with the kids of today is that they think they're invincible, they want everything in the here and now and forget about where they came from. Now, Jemima will definitely remember where she came from and what I did for her when she was little. It's only what I'm owed. Didn't I give up fifteen years of my life for the girl? Marnie Lake, ha, she's nothing but a joke.

I fill the glass again as I look for one of my shoes. I need to get ready to meet the girl. Can't wait to see her face… Now where's that other bloody shoe? My mobile buzzes. It's a text from Craig.

You know I care for you, Joyce, but this just doesn't feel right. Please don't go through with it. She's your daughter for god's sake. He's such a whiner, I can't believe he wants to back out on me.

Too late, Craig. You knew all along that this was the plan. I'm going ahead with it. More money for me, right, I quickly type back. Shame, I quite liked the man. If only he'd grown a pair.

I'm out. Finished. Have a good life.

Well, that's as clear as day then. I'm on my own again. I guess at some point he'll need to come back to get his belongings, I muse. Perhaps I can change his mind again…?

Ditto. I finish.

Now, onward and upward. I have a daughter to see and money to make. Phew, I see the elusive shoe poking out from under the bed and put it on. I then grab my stuff and rush out of the door to the car.

The traffic is surprisingly good as I pull into the car park at the Portland Bill lighthouse. I'm a few minutes late, but that's because I grabbed a Costa coffee through the drive-in to try and clear my head a little. Habitual drinkers are like anyone with an addiction, they learn how to live with it and supposedly function throughout the day. I've been drinking vodka back in my room since breakfast at the hotel at 8am. I feel a bit heady, a bit dazed, but don't feel too worried. Hopefully, the coffee will give me a bit of a punch.

I see Jemima leaning against a car, a takeaway coffee in her hand too. She walks toward me.

"Mother."

I hate it when she uses that tone with me. Like I'm some child who is constantly getting into trouble. She's the child here, right? This is how she presses my buttons, goading me and trying to make me feel inferior.

"Jemima."

"No Jemima darling, Mother? Is that just for show?"

113

"Damn right!" I can feel my blood boiling and my free hand balls into a fist. What I wouldn't give to be able to mark that pretty face with my fist. It would make my day. Keep calm, Joyce, don't give her the satisfaction.

Jemima moves toward a wooden bench and sits. I follow, and we sit in silence for a few minutes.

"I know why you need the money," she begins "You are behind with your mortgage payments."

"Yes." I force the word out.

"Why couldn't you have just asked me for the money?" she asks. For a moment I see hurt fleet across her face.

"Ask you for something! You've been the bane of my existence since you were born. Even your father left because he couldn't stand the sight of you!" I spit out. Hatred flows from my lips as I watch her face pale.

"I don't believe you, Mother," she says. "I don't know why he left but it wasn't because of me!" Almost there, I've got her where I want her. I take a slip of paper from my pocket on which I've written my bank account and sort code details.

"Here, you'll need this." I put the paper into her hand and fold her hand to keep it safe.

"I want £10,000 by midnight tonight. Or I start sharing confidential information wherever I can." I get up and walk back to my car without looking back. I can't help but smile. God, that was easy. Perhaps I'll treat myself to a pub meal and quick drink on the way back to celebrate. By tomorrow, I'll be a rich woman.

"There's not an ounce of goodness in you, is there?" Jemima's voice carries over the car park. "From this day on you are dead to me, do you hear!"

"At last!" I shout back. "She finally understands!" I get into the car and drive off.

Chapter 20:
The road to redemption: now (Jem)

I am such a fool for thinking that I would be able to talk to her, to make her see sense. How could she say that my father left us because of me? I was only four for pity's sake. It's just a game to her, this vicious game where she tries to destroy me to get what she wants. Her words cut me to the core. I sniffle. *No, don't let her do this to you again. You're stronger now, you understand that it's not your fault.* That the problem is hers and hers alone.

Someone shuffles toward me. It's Craig. I'm not sure why he is here, apart from spying on the unhappy reunion that I've just shared with my mother.

"Hey," he says as he sits down beside me on the bench.

"Hey." I stare at the floor feeling miserable. I just want a few minutes to myself. Is that too much to ask?

"I heard what she said to you. That wasn't nice."

"No, it wasn't. Nothing she ever says to me is nice."

"I'm sorry, Jem, so sorry. I didn't know what she was really like."

"That's okay, she's an expert in manipulating people to get what she wants."

Suddenly, I feel the need to offer Craig an olive branch, to give him a chance to be the person I know he wants to be. I think the time has come to share with him what really happened to me years ago. Whether it's right or wrong to do so I don't know, but something about Craig makes me think that he's been wronged by my mother too and that he deserves a second chance.

"There's something that I need to tell you. It started a long time ago when I was little." As though recounting a well-known childhood story, I tell Craig about my mother and how she treated me all those years ago. I told him that I left home at fifteen and that I met some good people along the way who became my new family. I also told him about Noah and Maureen and how they gave me something to hold on to before I left home.

When I finish telling him about my abusive childhood we sit in silence. He puts his hands on his face as though he's ashamed to look at me.

"Jesus, Jem," is all he says for the longest time. "I'm so pissed at Joyce, at what she did to you, is doing to you. How can you ever forgive me? How can I ever forgive myself, especially after calling you a slut? She deliberately used me to get to you. What a cow!"

He's distraught and angry as he sits with his head in his hands and his arms on his knees. I can't offer him any comfort, I haven't got anything left in me to give.

"I know," I say quietly. "But you've made a choice now, the right choice. You've distanced yourself from her. You can start again, build a new life."

"What about us?" he asks.

"I'm sorry, Craig, but I have all I want and need here with Noah. He's my forever."

"Are you sure? I mean, you've only really met each other again recently." I nod to show him that I'm totally sure of my future with Noah. Where else would I go? My home is here, it's been here all along, and I didn't realise it until I'd come back. My mother and Craig's actions put me on this road with their schemes and had unwittingly pushed me back where I needed to be.

"You're not the same people you were ten years ago. Despite that I want you to be happy, but if it's not with me then that's my loss," he says sadly.

"About this blackmail business." I broach the subject carefully, hoping that his road to redemption will continue a while longer. "Can you help? I need the photos, the laptop files, anything that Joyce has on The Lighthouse charity. I'm not bothered about me. Marnie Lake or Jemima Jenkins doesn't make a difference."

"I know where they are. I'll sort that out and delete everything." He's keen to help finish this unsavoury business.

"Thank you, Craig. I appreciate that." I hug him briefly to show my appreciation and to say my final goodbye. There's no feeling there, just a numbness that feels alien and mechanical at the same time.

"I'll let you know how I get on. Bye, Jem, and good luck with everything."

"You too."

I sit for a minute watching Craig walk away. His shoulders are slumped and his hands deep in his coat pockets. He heads for the battered Fiesta parked next to my Peugeot. He peers through the fully open window, leans in and says thoughtfully, "She's all yours, mate. Look after her, she deserves some happiness."

Noah nods. "Cheers."

I let Craig walk on a little toward the main road, shoulders slumped in defeat, then I stand up and start to walk slowly to the Fiesta.

"You okay?" Noah asks as he gets out of the car.

"I thought she was going to hit me at one point, but yeah, I'm okay." I need to touch him, need him to settle and calm me like he always does, so I reach out and put my hand over his heart. The quiet beats make a steady rhythmic pattern and I take in a sharp breath and sigh out the stress that's been building up inside me.

"I'm so proud of you," he whispers, his forehead touching mine. "How did you get to be so strong? No matter what that woman throws at you, you never stoop to her level."

"Craig's going to get rid of the blackmail evidence and software files. I'm hoping that there's nothing else up her sleeve to cause more trouble."

"I heard. I also heard what you said about us. About me being your forever." He kisses me on the cheek and takes both of my hands.

"It's true. I want to be here with you, with Maureen and close to Chloe, Jenny and the guys. I'll have to sort out my house in Frampton but I can paint anywhere. Let's enjoy today and this moment before dealing with the fallout. Besides, I think it's about time you finally ask me on a date," I smile.

"A date? I've already told you I love you! You'll be asking for a wedding ring next!" he says mockingly. I push him on the arm. Very funny. Honestly, what happened to taking things one day at a time? Still, the thought of marrying Noah makes my heart flutter and I feel overjoyed and overwhelmed at the same time.

"Chinese or Indian?"

"Chinese," I reply.

"Baby, we need to go home first. Gran texted me earlier to say that your stuff has arrived. We need to tell everyone what's happened and then I'm taking you out to dinner at a Chinese restaurant." "Baby". He called me baby! I can't help but smile.

"Sounds like a plan," I say, then I put my arms around his neck and kiss him like there's no tomorrow. Eventually we pull away and move towards our separate cars.

"See you back at base," he smiles.

I can't stop smiling as we both pull away and follow each other back to Maureen's.

Chapter 21:
A simple miscalculation: now
(Joyce)

This little pub is to die for. It's got twinkling lights in the garden which is great as darkness falls. There's a romantic aura as the lights shine over the landscaped gardens and outside dining furniture. It's posh, top of the range stuff. I'll have to get used to this when Jemima's money comes through. That reminds me to look at the time. My watch says 9pm as I silently remind myself to check my online banking at midnight.

I've been here for a couple of hours now and I've enjoyed good food and a couple of bottles of red wine. They've all gone down nicely with the earlier vodka drinks and left me feeling relaxed and chilled. Someone sits on the chair opposite me. He's dark skinned and a real hunk. This could be the start of my lucky streak.

"Sorry, I meant to ask first, but do you mind if I sit here?" he smiles.

"No, not at all," I say.

"I'm Gavin, but everyone calls me Gav," he says holding out his hand.

I take his hand in mine to shake. It's cool and firm.

"Joyce."

"Nice to meet you, Joyce."

"So, what do you do for a living, Gav?" I ask, wondering what opportunities this meeting might offer in my favour.

"I own an estate agent business in Weymouth."

"Oh, really? Sounds interesting."

"It is. Can I buy you a drink?" Can he buy me a drink? That's the question of the year. The best thing you can ask an alcoholic. I'll have a bottle of whisky please. Don't mind if I do.

"That would be nice. I'll have a whisky and soda please." I give him my brightest smile. The night is looking up.

Several drinks later and my watch says 10.30pm. I'm feeling a little flirty and tipsy. I stroke Gav's arm and tell him that I need to use the bathroom. I check my face and undo a button on my blouse. I take out my small plastic water bottle filled with vodka, take a quick sip, and then take one last look in the mirror to check my lipstick and push up my cleavage. Looking good for forty-six if I say so myself.

I head back to my table and Gav. There's no sign of him and I see a note under a half full whisky glass. As I get closer I read the note. *Sorry, Joyce, something cropped up. Dinner one night? Here's my number.* Bugger. Bugger. I swig back the drink, put the note in my bag and head to my car. Perhaps I'll have an early night after all.

My head feels a little heavy and my responses a little slow as I put the car into first gear. I'm sure my head will clear soon, I've drank more than this before now and felt fine. I start the journey around the dark unlit lanes towards the hotel. I swear it was a shorter distance than this on the way here, but I guess the dark makes it feel longer. I see a straight road ahead in the dark lane and pop on my full-beam headlights. Revving the car, I think about all the things I am going to do with the money and whether I will need future payments to support my lifestyle.

Suddenly, there's a tight bend in the road that I've miscalculated. I'm going too fast. I slam my feet on the brakes but I'm going too fast to slow sufficiently enough. The car hits something hard and I'm pushed forward through the windscreen, hanging half in and half out as the car twists and turns. The last thing I think of before everything goes dark is how thick the tree branch is that's heading for my face.

Chapter 22:
Karma: now (Jem)

We arrive at Maureen's almost at the same time and laughingly hold hands as Noah puts his key in the door. It's been a weird day, well, a couple of weird days really. There are voices in the living room. It's only 6pm but it feels much later. As we walk into the living room, Maureen rushes to me and gives me a hug. Jenny is on her phone and Stuart is quietly talking to someone on his.

"Thank god you're back. Everything okay with your mother?"

"Yes and no. She was her usual charming self. I couldn't change her mind."

Maureen looks at Noah and he nods to tell her that things are okay.

"Jack says hi, Jem," Stuart shouts.

"Hey, Jack," I call back.

"He couldn't find anything at the hotel. She must have hidden it."

"Can you put him on speaker, Stu?" I ask. Stuart presses a button and nods to me.

I sit on the arm of the sofa and explain what happened during the meeting and my conversation with Craig.

"Craig has cut ties with Mother and says that he will destroy all evidence containing information on The Lighthouse homes. I'm not bothered about the Marnie Lake thing. It is what it is, perhaps it's time to start afresh and be upfront anyway. I trust Craig, we had a good, honest conversation. He's going to let me know when he's gotten rid of everything."

There's a huge sigh of relief from everyone in the room. Noah is messing with his phone, I think he's trying to book a restaurant online.

"Sounds good, Jem. Let me know if I can help with anything else," Jack's voice calls out.

"Will do. Thanks, Jack." We all say our goodbyes and Jack hangs up.

"I am hopeful that this is the end of it. As soon as I hear from Craig I'll let you know. We should update Steph too." I slide off the arm of the sofa and shuffle next to Noah who's just sat down.

"I owe you all big time." I'm sincere as I look at each of my close friends. I really can't thank them all enough. They are my family and I will do anything to protect them. We chat for another couple of minutes until Noah stands.

"Right," he says, putting his hand out to me. I take it and he pulls me up to him. "Time for our date."

"Date?" the others say in unison.

"You're going on a date?" Jenny asks me. I simply nod and smile.

"About bloody time!" Maureen chimes in.

"Yep. Can't wait. I'm just going to quickly freshen up."

"Go on." He smacks my bottom softly. "Be quick, I'm hungry, babe!"

I giggle as I run upstairs.

Chapter 23:
Date night: now (Jem)

I put my napkin on my blue linen dress and twiddle with my necklace. Thank goodness my phone, clothes and toiletries from the hotel room arrived this afternoon or I would be dressed in one of Maureen's ensembles. I look across the table at Noah and butterflies immediately begin to work their way into my stomach. I cannot believe how nervous I feel. *It's Noah, just Noah. Stop panicking!*

"Are you nervous?" he asks.

"Yes," I say honestly. "You?"

"Yes," he reveals. "A little."

His hand lies on the table and I cover it with mine.

"I remember the first time I saw you. I was five. Your hair was loose and curly as you skipped around the playground with your friends. You were wearing a yellow checked school dress."

"I remember that!" I smile fondly remembering the dress. "I used to love that dress."

"You had a split lip and said you'd walked into the coffee table at home."

"Wasn't quick enough at that age to escape Mother's lashings after Dad left." A sudden overwhelming feeling of sorrow came over me. I don't know why. I'd faced a lot worse from Mother over the years. I guess it's the thought of the loss of a childhood or innocence that I can never replace which makes me feel this way. These repressed emotions occasionally catch up with me and I need to let them out, to allow myself time to grieve for everything that I had been through.

"Hey." He leans over, and his thumb gently traces my lower lip. "Don't. Don't let her win. She took most of your childhood and early teens. Don't let her take the rest of you."

"I'm sorry. This was supposed to be our date night," I whisper, and before I know what he's doing he leaves his chair and kneels beside me.

I'm engulfed in strong arms and a soft tickling whisper in my ear that says, "Oh, this is just the beginning, baby. I'm going to spend the rest of my life making sure that you understand what being loved is. Starting now." He kisses my lips gently and returns to his chair.

Wow! How does he do that? How does he know exactly how to calm and reassure me. This man loves me no matter what – unconditionally. How can that be? When did I get to be so lucky? I smile to myself as I think of Maureen's words. She knew all along. She knew I'd come back one day and that everything would work out. I just needed a reason to come home.

We order a variety of starters and mains to share and I'm enjoying a glass of red wine while Noah favours the driver's favourite, diet coke. My mobile buzzes and it's Craig to say that everything has been destroyed and deleted. Thank god for that. The boy did come through in the end. I let Maureen, Jenny, Noah and Steph know that things have been sorted.

"That's something to celebrate." Noah raises his glass and we clink. "It's almost over. I hope Joyce leaves you alone after this."

We have a lovely evening and Noah decides that it's time I saw his office and apartment, so we make a quick detour on the way home. I'm excited and a little nervous to see this part of Noah's life. The office is neat, tidy and inviting.

He offers his hand as we head up the stairs to his apartment. I slip my fingers through his and let him lead me into the open-plan space. It's gorgeous. Comfortable sofas and chairs are arranged at the far end of the room with a massive TV on the wall and different sized Alexa smart devices dotted around the apartment. There's a mantlepiece near one of the sofas and a dining area to one side. The kitchen is grey with white quartz worktops and there's a preparation island for communal cooking in the middle of the area. I love it. So modern but so totally lived in.

"Coffee? Another drink?" Noah asks, watching carefully for my reaction.

My attention focuses on the painting over the mantlepiece. It's one of mine, waves coming in from the sea onto the sand, *Free*, and tears well in my eyes. I look at Noah who just smiles and nods to the dining area. I slowly walk to the second painting, *Famous*, of the harbour at Lyme Regis.

He brings two coffee mugs over and hands me one.

"You, Jem," he says solemnly. "It was always you."

The moment is lost by my mobile ringing. Who's calling me so late? It's Craig. I answer the call.

"Jem. I'm sorry."

"Craig. What? What's happened?" A strange feeling overtakes me, as though someone has just walked over my grave.

"It's your mother. I've just come back from the hospital. They found my number alongside a note from someone called Gavin in her handbag. I don't know who he is but they asked me to identify her body. She was drinking, and she took a bend in the road too fast. She died in the ambulance."

"Dead," I repeat numbly. "Jesus, how can she be dead, I only saw her a few hours ago?" I look at Noah, who's shaking his head in disbelief.

Everything that I've been through over the years, every little thing over the last week, has been bringing me to this moment. My mother's death. I never wanted her dead, just away from me. I shouldn't be surprised that drink caused her accident in the end.

"Was anyone else involved?" I ask him, holding my breath. I couldn't bear it if her actions had injured or killed others.

"No. She was alone and thankfully no other vehicle was involved," he reveals as I slowly begin to breathe again. Thank god.

"Thanks for letting me know," I tell him and disconnect the line.

I walk to Noah's sofa and slump down. Well, that's something I wasn't expecting tonight, another curve ball, another shake of the lamp-post to work through and overcome. Noah sits next to me and slides his arm over my shoulder.

"She's dead," I say again.

"She can't hurt anyone ever again," he says, turning my face to his and we sit, still in shock, thinking about a woman who didn't know how to love or be loved, who had spent her whole life making people miserable or manipulating them.

Life is fickle. If there's anything I've learnt from the last couple of weeks, it's that you don't know what's around the corner, or what may happen in the next moment or years to come.

You need to take a leap of faith and live life to the full. Enjoy every moment and be the best person you can be, because we only have one chance at this life. For who knows when that moment will end? I think its karma that my mother died the way she did. What do you think?

Epilogue:
Three months later

My mother's funeral took place a week after her car accident. It was recorded as death by dangerous driving impeded by alcohol consumption. She was ten times over the legal limit.

I made myself attend her funeral and was flanked by those closest to me, including Noah and Maureen. Craig attended and sat in the pew opposite us. We acknowledged each other with a sad nod as we left the building. There was nothing left for us to say. It seems that Mother didn't have any friends or relatives which makes me wonder how someone can go through life without making any connections or relationships with people. I paid for the funeral and had her cremated. I've done my bit, paid my dues and I've now got closure. Time to move on, time to live.

"You look beautiful." Maureen looks at me with tears in her eyes. Her hand is on my shoulder gently reassuring me as I look at myself in the mirror. Yes, it's a new wedding dress. You didn't think I'd wear the old one, did you? It's plain silk ivory with a simple heart-shaped neckline.

My thoughts go back to a month ago when Noah asked me to marry him. We'd decided that it would be easier for Noah to move into my Frampton house as it was much bigger, so we were packing up his apartment. He'd been busy dissolving the practice partnership with Suzanne and she'd been busy leaning on his friend Charlie's shoulders for support. Chloe had been visiting for a few days and we had enjoyed catching up with the latest escapades of our lives. I particularly liked listening to how well she and Joel were getting on together. She deserves her fairy tale too and I have my fingers constantly crossed for her. I think I may need a wedding hat soon, it's just a feeling I keep getting! I'm digressing. I look up from wrapping plates in bubble wrap in the apartment to see Noah hovering with one of my old doodle books.

He's staring at a page. Now I'm worried. Solemnly he walks to me, holding the page open.

"I like this one of me the best," he says, pointing to an early sketch of him smiling as he looks at something in the distance. I glance at the page and smile. There's something shiny taped to the page and several Post-it notes attached to the paper. Noah's writing.

I take the book and read the three Post-its slowly.

I love you. You are my hope and my light. Will you marry me?

He smiles sheepishly at me as I pull the ring from the tape.

"It was my mother's. Gran kept it for me. It was always yours." I hold the white gold engagement ring with a twist knot and single diamond. It's beautiful. I put it on my finger. It's a little big but who cares? I throw myself at Noah.

"Yes! Yes! Yes!" I say, my voice quivering with emotion. "I love you, Noah, so much."

"I love you too, baby. Let's not waste any more time," he says kissing me with a passion that rivals my own.

"One stipulation though, I don't want a long engagement. You have a one month reprieve before I make you my wife. I'm happy to help with anything, but one month and then you're legally mine!"

I smile as I think of that moment when he told me that he couldn't wait for me to become his wife. I feel exactly the same way about him. Why should we wait?

Maureen's voice flows through my thoughts and brings me back to today and the reality of my wedding.

"I'm so proud of you both and the people you've become. I love you both so much." She sniffles through her smiles and dabs a tissue at her eye.

Jenny and Lottie rush into the room.

"The car's here," Jenny says.

They both stop in front of me for a second. The love we all share shines into the happy tears forming in our eyes.

"Gorgeous, sweetie, you look gorgeous," Lottie says as she and Jenny move in for a hug.

"Ok, let's get this show on the road. Right, I love you guys and will see you at the registry office soon." I motion for them all to go.

Chloe texts me. *No running this time, babe. Keep those trainers in the house! See you soon. Love you. xx* Ha! I laugh. She's so funny. I can't wait to see her relieved smiling face as I walk by her in the aisle!

Stuart has decorated his car with white wedding ribbon and is going to walk me down the aisle. We're really going to do this Noah and me. I've left the Peugeot at Maureen's so there's no chance of a quick getaway even if I wanted to, which I don't.

As I walk down the aisle flanked by friends and my adopted family members, I smile with the reassurance that this time it's for real. Noah in a dark grey suit suddenly turns to look at me and I forget to breathe. His eyes hold mine and his smile calms me.

I smile at Stuart and he kisses my cheek ready to hand me to Noah. I'm holding on to my bouquet of red roses for dear life. *I love you,* he mouths. *I love you,* I mouth back, throw my arms around him and kiss his cheek. There are a few giggles from behind me but I don't care. The registrar gives me a patient smile, I can tell that she wants to start her speech and get the ceremony started. I know it's not the right etiquette for a wedding, but this is my wedding and I'm the star of it, right?

Life is good.

Printed in Great Britain
by Amazon